Goosebumps®

Goosebumps®

THE HAUNTED MASK

R. L. STINE

SCHOLASTIC INC.

Goosebumps books created by Parachute Press, Inc.

Copyright © 1993 by Scholastic Inc.

All rights reserved. Published by Scholastic Inc., *Publishers since 1920*. SCHOLASTIC, GOOSEBUMPS, GOOSEBUMPS HORRORLAND, and associated logos are trademarks and/or registered trademarks of Scholastic Inc.

ISBN 978-0-590-49446-5

10   9   8   7   6   5   4   15   16   17   18   19

Printed in China 145
This edition first printing 2015

THE HAUNTED MASK

"What are you going to be for Halloween?" Sabrina Mason asked. She moved her fork around in the bright yellow macaroni on her lunch tray but didn't take a bite.

Carly Beth Caldwell sighed and shook her head. The overhead light on the lunchroom ceiling made her straight brown hair gleam. "I don't know. A witch, maybe."

Sabrina's mouth dropped open. "You? A witch?"

"Well, why not?" Carly Beth demanded, staring across the long table at her friend.

"I thought you were afraid of witches," Sabrina replied. She raised a forkful of macaroni to her mouth and started to chew. "This macaroni is made of rubber," she complained, chewing hard. "Remind me to start packing a lunch."

"I am *not* afraid of witches!" Carly Beth insisted, her dark eyes flashing angrily. "You just think I'm a big scaredy-cat, don't you!"

Sabrina giggled. "Yes." She flipped her black ponytail behind her shoulders with a quick toss of her head. "Hey, don't eat the macaroni. Really, Carly Beth. It's gross." She reached across the table to keep Carly Beth from raising her fork.

"But I'm *starving*!" Carly Beth complained.

The lunchroom grew crowded and noisy. At the next table, a group of fifth-grade boys were tossing a half-full milk carton back and forth. Carly Beth saw Chuck Greene ball up a bright red fruit rollup and shove the whole sticky thing in his mouth.

"Yuck!" She made a disgusted face at him. Then she turned back to Sabrina. "I am *not* a scaredycat, Sabrina. Just because everyone picks on me and —"

"Carly Beth, what about last week? Remember? At my house?" Sabrina ripped open a bag of tortilla chips and offered some across the table to her friend.

"You mean the ghost thing?" Carly Beth replied, frowning. "That was really stupid."

"But you believed it," Sabrina said with a mouthful of chips. "You really believed my attic was haunted. You should have seen the look on your face when the ceiling started to creak, and we heard the footsteps up there."

"That was so mean," Carly Beth complained, rolling her eyes.

2

"Then when you heard footsteps coming down the stairs, your face went all white and you screamed," Sabrina recalled. "It was only Chuck and Steve."

"You *know* I'm afraid of ghosts," Carly Beth said, blushing.

"And snakes and bugs and loud noises and dark rooms and — and witches!" Sabrina declared.

"I don't see why you have to make fun of me," Carly Beth pouted. She shoved her lunch tray away. "I don't see why everyone always thinks it's so much fun to try to scare me. Even you, my best friend."

"I'm sorry," Sabrina said sincerely. She reached across the table and squeezed Carly Beth's wrist reassuringly. "You're just so easy to scare. It's hard to resist. Here. Want some more chips?" She shoved the bag toward Carly Beth.

"Maybe I'll scare *you* some day," Carly Beth threatened.

Her friend laughed. "No way!"

Carly Beth continued to pout. She was eleven. But she was tiny. And with her round face and short stub of a nose (which she hated and wished would grow longer), she looked much younger.

Sabrina, on the other hand, was tall, dark, and sophisticated-looking. She had straight black hair tied behind her head in a ponytail and enormous dark eyes. Everyone who saw them together assumed that Sabrina was twelve or thirteen. But, actually, Carly Beth was a month older than her friend.

"Maybe I won't be a witch," Carly Beth said thoughtfully, resting her chin on her hands. "Maybe I'll be a disgusting monster with hanging eyeballs and green slime dripping down my face and —"

A loud crash made Carly Beth scream.

It took her a few seconds to realize that it was just a lunch tray hitting the floor. She turned to see Gabe Moser, his face bright red, drop to his knees and start scooping his lunch off the floor. The lunchroom rang out with cheers and applause.

Carly Beth hunched down in her seat, embarrassed that she had screamed.

Her breathing had just returned to normal when a strong hand grabbed her shoulder from behind.

Carly Beth's shriek echoed through the room.

She heard laughter. At another table, someone yelled, "Way to go, Steve!"

She whipped her head around to see her friend Steve Boswell standing behind her, a mischievous grin on his face. "Gotcha," he said, letting go of her shoulder.

Steve pulled out the chair next to Carly Beth's and lowered himself over its back. His best friend, Chuck Greene, slammed his book bag onto the table and then sat down next to Sabrina.

Steve and Chuck looked so much alike, they could have been brothers. Both were tall and thin, with straight brown hair, which they usually hid under baseball caps. Both had dark brown eyes and goofy grins. Both wore faded blue jeans and dark-colored, long-sleeved T-shirts.

And both of them loved to scare Carly Beth. They loved to startle her, to make her jump and shriek.

They spent hours dreaming up new ways to frighten her.

She vowed every time that she would never — *never* — fall for one of their stupid tricks again.

But so far, they had won every time.

Carly Beth always threatened to pay them back. But in all the time they'd been friends, she hadn't been able to think of anything good enough.

Chuck reached for the few remaining chips in Sabrina's bag. She playfully slapped his hand away. "Get your own."

Steve held a crinkled hunk of aluminum foil under Carly Beth's nose. "Want a sandwich? I don't want it."

Carly Beth sniffed it suspiciously. "What kind is it? I'm *starving*!"

"It's a turkey sandwich. Here," Steve said, handing it to Carly Beth. "It's too dry. My mom forgot the mayo. You want it?"

"Yeah, sure. Thanks!" Carly Beth exclaimed. She took the sandwich from him and peeled back the aluminum foil. Then she took a big bite of the sandwich.

As she started to chew, she realized that both Steve and Chuck were staring at her with big grins on their faces.

Something tasted funny. Kind of sticky and sour.

Carly Beth stopped chewing.

Chuck and Steve were laughing now. Sabrina looked confused.

Carly Beth uttered a disgusted groan and spit the chewed-up sandwich hunk into a napkin. Then she pulled the bread apart — and saw a big brown worm resting on top of the turkey.

"Ohh!" With a moan, she covered her face with her hands.

The room erupted with laughter. Cruel laughter.

"I ate a worm. I-I'm going to be sick!" Carly Beth groaned. She jumped to her feet and stared angrily at Steve. "How *could* you?" she demanded. "It isn't funny. It's — it's —"

"It isn't a real worm," Chuck said. Steve was laughing too hard to talk.

"Huh?" Carly Beth gazed down at it and felt a wave of nausea rise up from her stomach.

"It isn't real. It's rubber. Pick it up," Chuck urged.

Carly Beth hesitated.

Kids all through the vast room were whispering and pointing at her. And laughing.

"Go ahead. It isn't real. Pick it up," Chuck said, grinning.

Carly Beth reached down with two fingers and reluctantly picked the brown worm from the sandwich. It felt warm and sticky.

"Gotcha again!" Chuck said with a laugh.

It *was* real! A real worm!

With a horrified cry, Carly Beth tossed the worm at Chuck, who was laughing wildly. Then she leaped away from the table, knocking the chair over. As the chair clattered noisily against the hard floor, Carly Beth covered her mouth and ran gagging from the lunchroom.

I can still taste it! she thought.

I can still taste the worm in my mouth!

I'll pay them back for this, Carly Beth thought bitterly as she ran.

I'll pay them back. I really will.

As she pushed through the double doors and hurtled toward the girls' room, the cruel laughter followed her across the hall.

After school, Carly Beth hurried through the halls without talking to anyone. She heard kids laughing and whispering. She *knew* they were laughing at her.

Word had spread all over school that Carly Beth Caldwell had eaten a worm at lunch.

Carly Beth, the scaredy-cat. Carly Beth, who was frightened of her own shadow. Carly Beth, who was so easy to trick.

Chuck and Steve had sneaked a real worm, a fat brown worm, into a sandwich. And Carly Beth had taken a big bite.

What a jerk!

Carly Beth ran all the way home, three long blocks. Her anger grew with every step.

How could they do that to me? They're supposed to be my friends!

Why do they think it's so funny to scare me?

She burst into the house, breathing hard.

"Anybody home?" she called, stopping in the hallway and leaning against the banister to catch her breath.

Her mother hurried out from the kitchen. "Carly Beth! Hi! What's wrong?"

"I ran all the way," Carly Beth told her, pulling off her blue windbreaker.

"Why?" Mrs. Caldwell asked.

"Just felt like it," Carly Beth replied moodily.

Her mother took Carly Beth's windbreaker and hung it in the front closet for her. Then she brushed a hand affectionately through Carly Beth's soft brown hair. "Where'd you get the straight hair?" she muttered. Her mother was always saying that.

We don't look like mother and daughter at all, Carly Beth realized. Her mother was a tall, chubby woman with thick curls of coppery hair and lively gray-green eyes. She was extremely energetic, seldom stood still, and talked as rapidly as she moved.

Today she was wearing a paint-stained gray sweatshirt over black Lycra tights. "Why so grumpy?" Mrs. Caldwell asked. "Anything you'd care to talk about?"

Carly Beth shook her head. "Not really." She didn't feel like telling her mother that she had become the laughingstock of Walnut Avenue Middle School.

"Come here. I have something to show you," Mrs. Caldwell said, tugging Carly Beth toward the living room.

"I — I'm really not in the mood, Mom," Carly Beth told her, hanging back. "I just —"

"Come *on!*" her mother insisted, and pulled her across the hallway. Carly Beth always found it impossible to argue with her mother. She was like a hurricane, sweeping everything in her direction.

"Look!" Mrs. Caldwell declared, grinning and gesturing to the mantelpiece.

Carly Beth followed her mother's gaze to the mantel — and cried out in surprise. "It's — a head!"

"Not just *any* head," Mrs. Caldwell said, beaming. "Go on. Take a closer look."

Carly Beth took a few steps toward the mantelpiece, her eyes on the head staring back at her. It took her a few moments to recognize the straight brown hair, the brown eyes, the short snip of a nose, the round cheeks. "It's *me!*" she cried, walking up to it.

"Yes. Life-size!" Mrs. Caldwell declared. "I just came from my art class at the museum. I finished it today. What do you think?"

Carly Beth picked it up and studied it closely. "It looks just like me, Mom. Really. What's it made of?"

"Plaster of Paris," her mother replied, taking it from Carly Beth and holding it up so that Carly Beth was face to face, eye to eye with herself. "You have to be careful. It's delicate. It's hollow, see?"

Carly Beth stared intently at the head, peering into her own eyes. "It — it's kind of creepy," she muttered.

"You mean because I did such a good job?" her mother demanded.

"It's just creepy, that's all," Carly Beth said. She forced herself to look away from the replica of herself and saw that her mother's smile had faded.

Mrs. Caldwell looked hurt. "Don't you like it?"

"Yeah. Sure. It's really good, Mom," Carly Beth answered quickly. "But, I mean, why on earth did you make it?"

"Because I love you," Mrs. Caldwell replied curtly. "Why else? Honestly, Carly Beth, you have the strangest reactions to things. I worked really hard on this sculpture. I thought —"

"I'm sorry, Mom. I like it. Really, I do," Carly Beth insisted. "It was just a surprise, that's all. It's great. It looks just like me. I — I had a bad day, that's all."

Carly Beth took another long look at the sculpture. Its brown eyes — *her* brown eyes — stared back at her. The brown hair shimmered in the afternoon sunlight through the window.

It smiled at me! Carly Beth thought, her mouth dropping open. *I saw it! I just saw it smile!*

No. It had to be a trick of the light.

It was a plaster of Paris head, she reminded herself.

Don't go scaring yourself over nothing, Carly Beth. Haven't you made a big enough fool of yourself today?

"Thanks for showing it to me, Mom," she said awkwardly, pulling her eyes away. She forced a smile. "Two heads are better than one, right?"

"Right," Mrs. Caldwell agreed brightly. "Incidentally, Carly Beth, your duck costume is all ready. I put it on your bed."

"Huh? Duck costume?"

"You saw a duck costume at the mall, remember?" Mrs. Caldwell carefully placed the sculpted head on the mantel. "The one with all the feathers and everything. You thought it would be funny to be a duck this Halloween. So I made you a duck costume."

"Oh. Right," Carly Beth said, her mind spinning. *Do I really want to be a stupid duck this Halloween?* she thought. "I'll go up and take a look at it, Mom. Thanks."

Carly Beth had forgotten all about the duck costume. *I don't want to be cute this Halloween,* she thought as she climbed the stairs to her room. *I want to be scary.*

She had seen some really scary-looking masks

in the window of a new party store that had opened a few blocks from school. One of them, she knew, would be perfect.

But now she'd have to walk around in feathers and have everyone quack at her and make fun of her.

It wasn't fair. Why did her mother have to listen to every word she said?

Just because Carly Beth had admired a duck costume in a store didn't mean she wanted to be a stupid duck for Halloween!

Carly Beth hesitated outside her bedroom. The door had been pulled closed for some reason. She never closed the door.

She listened carefully. She thought she heard someone breathing on the other side of the door. Someone or some*thing.*

The breathing grew louder.

Carly Beth pressed an ear to the door.

What was in her room?

There was only one way to find out.

Carly Beth pulled open the door — and uttered a startled cry.

"QUAAAAAAACCCK!"

With a hideous cry, an enormous white-feathered duck, its eyes wild and frenzied, leaped at Carly Beth.

As she staggered backwards in astonishment, the duck knocked her over and pinned her to the hallway floor.

"QUAAACCCK! QUAAAACK!"

The costume has come alive!

That was Carly Beth's first frightened thought.

Then she quickly realized the truth. "Noah — get off me!" she demanded, trying to push the big duck off her chest.

The white feathers brushed against her nose. "Hey — that tickles!"

She sneezed.

"Noah — come *on!*"

"QUAAAAACCCK!"

"Noah, I mean it!" she told her eight-year-old brother. "What are you doing in my costume? It's supposed to be *my* costume."

"I was just trying it on," Noah said, his blue eyes staring down at her through the white-and-yellow duck mask. "Did I scare you?"

"Not a bit," Carly Beth lied. "Now get up! You're heavy!"

He refused to budge.

"Why do you always want everything that's mine?" Carly Beth demanded angrily.

"I don't," he replied.

"And why do you think it's so funny to try to scare me all the time?" she asked.

"I can't help it if you get scared every time I say *boo*," he replied nastily.

"Get up! Get up!"

He quacked a few more times, flapping the feathery wings. Then he climbed to his feet. "Can I have this costume? It's really neat."

Carly Beth frowned and shook her head. "You got feathers all over me. You're molting!"

"Molting? What's *that* mean?" Noah demanded. He pulled off the mask. His blond hair was damp from sweat and matted against his head.

"It means you're going to be a bald duck!" Carly Beth told him.

"I don't care. Can I have this costume?" Noah asked, examining the mask. "It fits me. Really!"

16

"I don't know," Carly Beth told him. "Maybe." The phone rang in her room. "Get lost, okay? Go fly south for the winter or something," she said, and hurried to answer the phone.

As she ran to her desk, she saw white feathers all over her bed. *That costume will never survive till Halloween!* she thought.

She picked up the receiver. "Hello? Oh, hi, Sabrina. Yeah. I'm okay."

Sabrina had called to remind Carly Beth that the school Science Fair was tomorrow. They had to finish their project, a model of the solar system constructed with Ping-Pong balls.

"Come over after dinner," Carly Beth told her. "It's almost finished. We just have to paint it. My mom said she'd help us take it to school tomorrow."

They chatted for a while. Then Carly Beth confided, "I was so mad, Sabrina. At lunch today. Why do Chuck and Steve think it's so funny to do things like that to me?"

Sabrina was silent for a moment. "I guess it's because you're so *scare-able*, Carly Beth."

"Scare-able?"

"You scream so easily," Sabrina said. "Other people get scared. But they're more quiet about it. You know Chuck and Steve. They don't really mean to be mean. They just think it's funny."

"Well, I *don't* think it's funny at all," Carly Beth

replied unhappily. "And I'm not going to be *scareable* anymore. I mean it. I'm *not* ever going to scream or get frightened again."

The science projects were all set up for judging on the stage in the auditorium. Mrs. Armbruster, the principal, and Mr. Smythe, the science teacher, walked from display to display, making notes on their clipboards.

The solar system, as designed by Carly Beth and Sabrina, had survived the trip to school in pretty good shape. Jupiter had a slight dent in it, which the girls had struggled unsuccessfully to straighten out. And Earth kept coming loose from its string and bouncing across the floor. But both girls agreed the display looked pretty good.

Maybe it wasn't as impressive as Martin Goodman's project. Martin had built a computer from scratch. But Martin was a genius. And Carly Beth figured the judges didn't expect everyone else to be geniuses, too.

Looking around the crowded, noisy stage, Carly Beth saw other interesting projects. Mary Sue Chong had built some kind of electronic robot arm that could pick up a cup or wave to people. And Brian Baldwin had several glass bottles filled with brown gunky stuff that he claimed was toxic waste.

Someone had done a chemical analysis of the town's drinking water. And someone had built a volcano that would erupt when the two judges came by.

"Our project is kind of boring," Sabrina whispered nervously to Carly Beth, her eyes on the two judges who were *oohing* and *aahing* over Martin Goodman's homemade computer. "I mean, it's just painted Ping-Pong balls on strings."

"I like our project," Carly Beth insisted. "We worked hard on it, Sabrina."

"I know," Sabrina replied fretfully. "But it's still kind of boring."

The volcano erupted, sending up a gusher of red liquid. The judges appeared impressed. Several kids cheered.

"Uh-oh. Here they come," Carly Beth whispered, jamming her hands into her jeans pockets. Mrs. Armbruster and Mr. Smythe, smiles plastered across their faces, were coming closer.

They stopped to examine a display of light and crystals.

Suddenly, Carly Beth heard an excited shout from somewhere behind her on the stage. "My tarantula! Hey — my tarantula got out!"

She recognized Steve's voice.

"Where's my tarantula?" he called.

Several kids uttered startled cries. Some kids laughed.

I'm not going to get scared, Carly Beth told herself, swallowing hard.

She knew she was terrified of tarantulas. But this time she was determined not to show it.

"My tarantula — it got away!" Steve shouted over the roar of excited voices.

I'm not going to get scared. I'm not going to get scared, Carly Beth repeated to herself.

But then she felt something pinch the back of her leg and dig its spiny pincer into her skin — and Carly Beth uttered a shrill scream of terror that rang out through the auditorium.

Carly Beth screamed and knocked over the solar system.

She kicked her leg wildly, trying to toss off the tarantula. Ping-Pong ball planets bounced over the floor.

She screamed again. "Get it off me! Get it *off*!"

"Carly Beth — stop!" Sabrina pleaded. "You're okay! You're okay!"

It took Carly Beth a long while to realize that everyone was laughing. Her heart pounding, she spun around to find Steve down on his hands and knees behind her.

He made a pinching motion with his thumb and finger. "Gotcha again," he said, grinning up at her.

"Noooo!" Carly Beth cried.

There was no tarantula, she realized. Steve had pinched her leg.

She raised her head and saw that kids all over the stage were laughing. Mrs. Armbruster and Mr. Smythe were laughing, too.

With a cry of anger, Carly Beth tried to kick Steve in the side. But he spun away. She missed.

"Help me pick up the planets," she heard Sabrina say.

But Sabrina seemed far, far away.

All Carly Beth could hear were the pounding of her heart and the laughter of the kids all around her. Steve had climbed to his feet. He and Chuck were side by side, grinning at her, slapping each other high fives.

"Carly Beth — help me," Sabrina pleaded.

But Carly Beth turned around, jumped off the stage, and ran, escaping up the dark auditorium aisle.

I'm going to pay Steve and Chuck back, she vowed angrily, her sneakers thudding loudly up the concrete aisle. *I'm going to scare them, REALLY scare them!*

But how?

"Okay. What time should I meet you?" Carly Beth asked, cradling the phone between her chin and shoulder.

On the other end of the line, Sabrina considered for a moment. "How about seven-thirty?"

It was Halloween. The plan was to meet at Sabrina's house, then go trick-or-treating through the entire neighborhood.

"The earlier the better. We'll get more candy," Sabrina said. "Did Steve call you?"

"Yeah. He called," Carly Beth replied bitterly.

"Did he apologize?"

"Yeah, he apologized," Carly Beth muttered, rolling her eyes. "Big deal. I mean, he already made me look like a jerk in front of the entire school. What good is an apology?"

"I think he felt bad," Sabrina replied.

"I *hope* he felt bad!" Carly Beth exclaimed. "It was so mean!"

"It was a dirty trick," Sabrina agreed. And then she added, "But you'll have to admit it was kind of funny."

"I don't have to admit anything!" Carly Beth snapped.

"Has it stopped raining?" Sabrina asked, changing the subject.

Carly Beth pulled back the curtain to glance out her bedroom window. The evening sky was charcoal-gray. Dark clouds hovered low. But the rain had stopped. The street glistened wetly under the light of a streetlamp.

"No rain. I've got to go. See you at seven-thirty," Carly Beth said, speaking rapidly.

"Hey, wait. What's your costume?" Sabrina demanded.

"It's a surprise," Carly Beth told her, and hung up.

It'll be a surprise to me, too, she told herself, glancing unhappily at the feathery duck costume rolled up on the chair in the corner.

Carly Beth's plan had been to go to the new party store after school and pick out the ugliest, most disgusting, scariest mask they had. But her mother had picked her up after school and insisted that she stay home and watch Noah for a couple of hours.

Mrs. Caldwell hadn't returned home until five-fifteen. Now it was nearly a quarter till six. *There was no way the party store would still be open,*

Carly Beth thought, frowning at the duck costume.

"Quack quack," she said miserably.

She walked to the mirror and ran a hairbrush through her hair. *Maybe it's worth a try,* she thought. *Maybe that store stays open late on Halloween.*

She pulled open her top dresser drawer and took out her wallet. Did she have enough money for a good, scary mask?

Thirty dollars. Her life savings.

She wadded up the bills and stuffed them back into the wallet. Then, jamming the wallet into her jeans pocket, she grabbed her coat and hurried downstairs and out the front door.

The evening air was cold and damp. Carly Beth struggled to zip her coat as she jogged toward the party store. The house next door had a glowing jack-o'-lantern in the front window. The house on the corner had paper skeletons strung up across the front porch.

The wind howled through the bare trees. The branches above her head shook and rattled like bony arms.

What a creepy night, Carly Beth thought.

She started running a little faster. A car rolled silently by, sending harsh white light floating across the sidewalk like a bright ghost.

Glancing across the street, Carly Beth saw the

old Carpenter mansion looming over its dark, weed-choked lawn. Everyone said the ramshackle old house was haunted by people who had been murdered inside it a hundred years ago.

Once, Carly Beth had heard frightening howls coming from the old mansion. When she was Noah's age, Steve and Chuck and some other kids had dared each other to go up to the house and knock on the door. Carly Beth had run home instead. She never did find out if the other kids were brave enough to do it.

Now Carly Beth felt a chill of fear as she hurried past the old house. She knew this neighborhood really well. She had lived in it her entire life. But tonight it looked different to her.

Was it just the wet glow left by the rain?

No. It was a heavy feeling in the air. A heavier darkness. The eerie orange glow of grinning pumpkins in windows. The silent cries of ghouls and monsters waiting to float free on their night to celebrate. Halloween.

Trying to force all the scary thoughts from her mind, Carly Beth turned the corner. The little party store came into view. The window was lighted, revealing two rows of Halloween masks, staring out at the street.

But was the store still open?

Crossing her fingers, Carly Beth waited for a truck to rumble past, then eagerly jogged across the street. She stopped for a second to examine the masks in the window. There were gorilla masks, monster masks, some sort of blue-haired alien mask.

Pretty good, she thought. *These are pretty ugly. But they probably have even scarier ones inside.*

The lights were on in the store. She peered through the glass door. Then she tried turning the knob.

It didn't move.

She tried again. She tried pulling the door open. Then she tried pushing.

No. No way.

She was too late. The store was closed.

Carly Beth sighed and peered in through the glass. The walls of the tiny store were covered with masks. The masks seemed to stare back at her.

They're laughing at me, she thought unhappily. *Laughing at me because I'm too late. Because the store is closed, and I'm going to have to be a stupid duck for Halloween.*

Suddenly, a dark shadow moved over the glass, blocking Carly Beth's view. She gasped and took a step back.

It took her a moment to realize that the shadow was a man. A man in a black suit, staring out at her, a look of surprise on his face.

"Are you — are you closed?" Carly Beth shouted through the glass.

The man gestured that he couldn't hear her. He turned the lock and pulled the door open an inch. "Can I help you?" he asked curtly. He had shiny black hair, parted in the middle and slicked down on his head, and a pencil-thin black mustache.

"Are you open?" Carly Beth asked timidly. "I need a Halloween mask."

"It's very late," the man replied, not answering her question. He pulled the door open another few inches. "We normally close at five."

"I really would like to buy a mask," Carly Beth told him in her most determined voice.

The man's tiny black eyes peered into hers. His expression remained blank. "Come in," he said quietly.

As Carly Beth stepped past him into the store, she saw that he wore a black cape. *It must be a Halloween costume*, she told herself. *I'm sure he doesn't wear that all the time.*

She turned her attention to the masks on the two walls.

"What kind of mask are you looking for?" the man asked, closing the door behind him.

Carly Beth felt a stab of fear. His black eyes glowed like two burning coals. He seemed so strange. And here she was, locked in this closed store with him.

"A s-scary one," she stammered.

He rubbed his chin thoughtfully. He pointed to the wall. "The gorilla mask has been very popular. It has real hair. I believe I may have one left in stock."

Carly Beth stared up at the gorilla mask. She didn't really want to be a gorilla. It was too ordinary. It wasn't scary enough. "Hmmm . . . do you have anything scarier?" she asked.

He flipped his cape back over the shoulder of his black suit. "How about that yellowish one with the pointy ears?" he suggested, pointing. "I believe it's some sort of *Star Trek* character. I still have a few of them, I believe."

"No." Carly Beth shook her head. "I need something really scary."

A strange smile formed under the man's thin mustache. His eyes burned into hers, as if trying to read her thoughts. "Look around," he said with a sweep of his hand. "Everything I have left in stock is up on the walls."

Carly Beth turned her gaze to the masks. A pig mask with long ugly tusks and blood trickling from the snout caught her eye. *Pretty good,* she thought. *But not quite right.*

A hairy werewolf mask with white pointy fangs was hung beside it. Again, too ordinary, Carly Beth decided.

Her eyes glanced over a green Frankenstein mask, a Freddy Kreuger mask that came with Freddy's hand — complete with long silvery blades for fingers — and an E.T. mask.

Just not scary enough, Carly Beth thought, starting to feel a little desperate. *I need something that will really make Steve and Chuck die of fright!*

"Young lady, I am afraid I must ask you to make your choice," the man in the cape said softly. He had moved behind the narrow counter at the front and was turning a key in the cash register. "We really are closed, after all."

"I'm sorry," Carly Beth started. "It's just that —"

The phone rang before she could finish explaining.

The man picked it up quickly and began talking in a low voice, turning his back to Carly Beth.

She wandered toward the back of the store, studying the masks as she walked. She passed a black cat mask with long, ugly yellow fangs. A vampire mask with bright red blood trickling down its lips was hung next to a grinning bald mask of Uncle Fester from *The Addams Family*.

Not right, not right, not right, Carly Beth thought, frowning.

She hesitated when she spotted a narrow door slightly opened at the back of the store. Was there another room? Were there more masks back there?

She glanced to the front. The man, hidden behind his cape, still had his back to her as he talked on the phone.

Carly Beth gave the door a hesitant push to peek inside. The door creaked open. Pale orange light washed over the small shadowy back room.

Carly Beth stepped inside — and gasped in amazement.

Two dozen empty eye sockets stared blindly at Carly Beth.

She gaped in horror at the distorted, deformed faces.

They were masks, she realized. Two shelves of masks. But the masks were so ugly, so grotesque — so *real* — they made her breath catch in her throat.

Carly Beth gripped the doorframe, reluctant to enter the tiny back room. Staring into the dim orange light, she studied the hideous masks.

One mask had long, stringy yellow hair falling over its bulging green forehead. A hairy black rat's head poked up from a knot in the hair, the rat's eyes gleaming like two dark jewels.

The mask beside it had a large nail stuck through an eyehole. Thick, wet-looking blood poured from the eye, down the cheek.

Chunks of rotting skin appeared to be falling off another mask, revealing gray bone underneath.

An enormous black insect, some kind of grotesque beetle, poked out from between the green-and-yellow decayed teeth.

Carly Beth's horror mixed with excitement. She took a step into the room. The wooden floorboards creaked noisily beneath her.

She took another step closer to the grotesque, grinning masks. They seemed so real, so horribly real. The faces had such detail. The skin appeared to be made of flesh, not rubber or plastic.

These are perfect! she thought, her heart pounding. *These are just what I was looking for. They look* terrifying *just propped up on these shelves!*

She imagined Steve and Chuck seeing one of these masks coming at them in the dark of night. She pictured herself uttering a bloodcurdling scream and leaping out from behind a tree in one of them.

She imagined the horrified expressions on the boys' faces. She pictured Steve and Chuck shrieking in terror and running for their lives.

Perfect. Perfect!

What a laugh that would be. What a victory!

Carly Beth took a deep breath and stepped up to the shelves. Her eyes settled on an ugly mask on the lower shelf.

It had a bulging bald head. Its skin was a putrid yellow-green. Its enormous sunken eyes were an eerie orange and seemed to glow. It had a broad, flat nose smashed in like a skeleton's nose. The dark-lipped mouth gaped wide, revealing jagged animal fangs.

Staring hard at the hideous mask, Carly Beth reached out a hand toward it. Reluctantly, she touched the broad forehead.

And as she touched it, the mask cried out.

"Ohh!"

Carly Beth shrieked and jerked back her hand.

The mask grinned at her. Its orange eyes glowed brightly. The lips appeared to curl back over the fangs.

She suddenly felt dizzy. *What is going on here?*

As she staggered back, away from the shelves, she realized that the angry cry hadn't come from the mask.

It had come from behind her.

Carly Beth spun around to see the black-caped store owner glaring at her from the doorway. His dark eyes flashed. His mouth was turned down into a menacing frown.

"Oh. I thought —" Carly Beth started, glancing back at the mask. She still felt confused. Her heart pounded loudly in her chest.

"I am sorry you saw these," the man said in a low, threatening voice. He took a step toward her, his cape brushing the doorway.

What is he going to do? Carly Beth wondered, uttering a horrified gasp. *Why is he coming at me like that?*

What is he going to do to me?

"I am so sorry," he repeated, his small dark eyes burning into hers. He took another step closer.

Carly Beth backed away from him. Then she uttered a startled cry as she backed into the display shelves.

The hideous masks jiggled and quaked, as if alive.

"What — what do you mean?" she managed to choke out. "I — I was just —"

"I am sorry you saw these because they are not for sale," the man said softly.

He stepped past her and straightened one of the masks on its stand.

Carly Beth breathed a loud sigh of relief. *He didn't mean to scare me,* she told herself. *I am scaring myself.*

She crossed her arms in front of her coat and tried to force her heartbeat to return to normal. She stepped to the side as the store owner continued to arrange the masks, handling them carefully, brushing their hair with one hand, tenderly dusting off their bulging, blood-covered foreheads.

"Not for sale? Why not?" Carly Beth demanded. Her voice came out tiny and shrill.

36

"Too scary," the man replied. He turned to smile at her.

"But I want a really scary one," Carly Beth told him. "I want *that* one." She pointed to the mask she had touched, the mask with the open mouth and its terrifying jagged fangs.

"Too scary," the man repeated, pushing his cape behind his shoulder.

"But it's Halloween!" Carly Beth protested.

"I have a really scary gorilla mask," the man said, motioning for Carly Beth to go back to the front room. "Very scary. Looks like it's growling. I will give you a good price on it since it's so late."

Carly Beth shook her head, her arms crossed defiantly in front of her. "Like I said before, a gorilla mask won't do. It won't scare Steve and Chuck," she said.

The man's expression changed. "Who?"

"My friends," she told him. "I *have* to have that one," she insisted. "It's so scary, I'm almost afraid to touch it. It's perfect."

"It's too scary," the man repeated, lowering his eyes to it. He ran his hand over the green forehead. "I can't take the responsibility."

"It's so real looking!" Carly Beth gushed. "They'll both faint. I know they will. Then they'll never try to scare me again."

"Young lady —" the store owner started, glancing impatiently at his watch. "I really must insist that you make up your mind. I am a patient man, but —"

"Please!" Carly Beth begged. "Please sell it to me! Here. Look." She dug into her jeans pocket and pulled out the money she had brought.

"Young lady, I —"

"Thirty dollars," Carly Beth said, shoving the wadded-up bills into the man's hand. "I'll give you thirty dollars for it. That's enough, isn't it?"

"It's not a matter of money," he told her. "These masks are not for sale." With an exasperated sigh, he started toward the doorway that led to the front of the store.

"Please! I *need* it. I really *need* it!" Carly Beth begged, chasing after him.

"These masks are too real," he insisted, gesturing to the shelves. "I'm warning you —"

"Please? Please?"

He shut his eyes. "You will be sorry."

"No, I won't. I won't. I *know* I won't!" Carly Beth exclaimed gleefully, seeing that he was about to give in.

He opened his eyes. He shook his head. She could see that he was debating with himself.

With a sigh, he tucked the money into his coat pocket. Then he carefully lifted the mask from the shelf, straightening the pointed ears, and started to hand it to her.

"Thanks!" she cried, eagerly snatching the mask from his hands. "It's perfect! Perfect!"

She held the mask by the flat nose. It felt soft and surprisingly warm. "Thanks again!" she cried, hurrying to the front, the mask gripped tightly in her hand.

"Can I give you a bag for it?" the man called after her.

But Carly Beth was already out of the store.

She crossed the street and started to run toward home. The sky was black. No stars poked through. The street still glistened wetly from the afternoon's rain.

This is going to be the best trick-or-treat night ever, Carly Beth thought happily. *Because this is the night I get my revenge.*

She couldn't wait to spring out at Steve and Chuck. She wondered what their costumes would be. They had both talked about painting their faces blue and dyeing their hair blue and being Smurfs.

Lame. Really lame.

Carly Beth stopped under a streetlight and held up the mask, gripping it with both hands by its pointed ears. It grinned up at her, the two crooked rows of fangs hanging over its thick, rubbery lips.

Then, tucking it carefully under one arm, she ran the rest of the way home.

Stopping at the bottom of the driveway, she gazed up at her house, the front windows all glowing brightly, the porchlight sending white light over the lawn.

I've got to try this mask out on someone, she thought eagerly. *I've got to see just how good it is.*

Her brother's grinning face popped into her mind.

"Noah. Of course," she said aloud. "Noah has really been asking for it."

Grinning gleefully, Carly Beth hurried up the driveway, eager to make Noah her first victim.

Carly Beth crept silently through the front door and tossed her coat onto the entryway floor. The house felt stuffy and hot. A sweet smell, the aroma of hot cider on the stove, greeted her.

Mom really gets into holidays, she thought with a smile.

Tiptoeing through the front hallway, holding the mask in front of her, Carly Beth listened hard.

Noah, where are you?

Where are you, my little guinea pig?

Noah was always bragging about how he was so much braver than Carly Beth. He was always putting bugs down her back and planting rubber snakes in her bed — anything he could think of to make her scream.

She heard footsteps above her head. *Noah must be up in his room,* she realized. *He's probably putting on his Halloween costume.*

At the last minute, Noah had decided he wanted

to be a cockroach. Mrs. Caldwell had dashed frantically all over the house, finding the materials to build pointy feelers and a hard shell for his back.

Well, the little bug is in for a surprise, Carly Beth thought evilly. She examined her mask. *This should send that cockroach scampering under the sink!*

She stopped at the bottom of the stairs. She could hear loud music coming from Noah's room. An old heavy-metal song.

Gripping the mask by the rubbery neck, she raised it carefully over her head, then pulled it slowly down.

It was surprisingly warm inside. The mask fit tighter than Carly Beth had imagined. It had a funny smell, kind of sour, kind of old, like damp newspapers that have been left for years in an attic or garage.

She slid it all the way down until she could see through the eyeholes. Then she smoothed the bulging bald head over her head and tugged the neck down.

I should have stopped in front of a mirror, she fretted. *I can't see if it looks right.*

The mask felt very tight. Her breathing echoed noisily in the flat nose. She forced herself to ignore the sour smell that invaded her nose.

She held on tightly to the banister as she crept up the stairs. It was hard to see the steps through the eyeholes. She had to take the climb slowly, one step at a time.

The heavy-metal music ended as she stepped onto the landing. She crept silently down the hall and stopped outside Noah's door.

Carly Beth edged her head into the doorway and peeked into the brightly lit room. Noah was standing in front of the mirror, adjusting the two long cockroach feelers above his head.

"Noah — I'm coming for you!" Carly Beth called.

To her surprise, her voice came out gruff and low. It wasn't her voice at all!

"Huh?" Startled, Noah spun around.

"Noah — I've *got* you!" Carly Beth shrieked, her voice deep, raspy, evil.

"No!" Her brother uttered a hushed cry of protest. Even under his bug makeup, Carly Beth could see him go pale.

She darted into the room, her arms outstretched as if ready to grab him.

"No — *please!*" he cried, his expression terrified. "Who *are* you? How — how did you get in?"

He doesn't even recognize me! Carly Beth thought gleefully.

And he's scared to death!

Was it the hideous face? The deep rumble of a voice? Or both?

Carly Beth didn't care. The mask was *definitely* a success!

"I've *GOT* you!" she screamed, surprising herself at how scary her voice sounded from inside the mask.

"No! Please!" Noah begged. "Mom! *Mom!*" He backed toward the bed, trembling all over, his feelers quivering in fright. "Mom! *Hellllp!*"

Carly Beth burst out laughing. The laughter came out in a deep rumble. "It's me, stupid!" she cried. "What a yellow-bellied scaredy-cat!"

"Huh?" Still huddled by the bed, Noah stared hard at her.

"Don't you recognize my jeans? My sweater? It's me, you idiot!" Carly Beth declared in the gruff voice.

"But your face — that mask!" Noah stammered. "It — it really scared me. I mean —" He gaped at her, studying the mask. "It didn't sound like you, Carly Beth," he muttered. "I thought —"

Carly Beth tugged at the bottom of the mask, trying to lift it off. It felt hot and sticky. She was panting noisily.

She tried pulling the bottom with both hands. The mask didn't budge.

She raised her hands to the pointed ears and tried lifting it off. She tugged. Tugged harder.

She tried pulling the mask off by the top of the head. It didn't move.

"Hey — it won't come off!" she cried. "The mask — it won't come off!"

"What's going on here?" Carly Beth cried, tugging at the mask with both hands.

"Stop it!" Noah cried. His voice sounded angry, but his eyes revealed fear. "Stop kidding around, Carly Beth. You're scaring me!"

"I'm *not* kidding around," Carly Beth insisted in her harsh, raspy voice. "I really can't — get — this — off!"

"Take it off! You're not funny!" her brother shouted.

With great effort, Carly Beth managed to slip her fingers under the neck of the mask. Then she pulled it away from her skin and lifted it off her head.

"Whew!"

The air felt so cool and sweet. She shook her hair free. Then she playfully tossed the mask at Noah. "Good mask, huh?" She grinned at him.

He let the mask bounce onto the bed. Then he

picked it up hesitantly and examined it. "Where'd you get it?" he asked, poking a finger against the ugly fangs.

"At that new party store," she told him, wiping perspiration from her forehead. "It's so hot inside it."

"Can I try it on?" Noah asked, pushing his fingers through the eyeholes.

"Not now. I'm late," she replied sharply. She laughed. "You sure looked scared."

He tossed the mask back at her, frowning. "I was just pretending," he said. "I knew it was you."

"For sure!" she replied, rolling her eyes. "That's why you screamed like a maniac."

"I did *not* scream," Noah protested. "I was just putting on an act. For you."

"Yeah. Right," Carly Beth muttered. She turned and headed toward the door, rolling the mask over her hand.

"How'd you change your voice like that?" Noah called after her.

Carly Beth stopped at the doorway and turned back to him. Her smile gave way to a puzzled expression.

"That deep voice was the scariest part," Noah said, staring at the mask in her hand. "How did you do that?"

"I don't know," Carly Beth replied thoughtfully. "I really don't know."

* * *

By the time she got to her room, she was grinning again. The mask had worked. It had been a wonderful success.

Noah might not want to admit it, but when Carly Beth burst in on him, growling through the hideous mask, he nearly jumped out of his cockroach shell.

Look out, Chuck and Steve! she thought gleefully. *You're next!*

She sat down on her bed and glanced at the clock radio on her bed table. She had a few minutes until it was time to meet everyone in front of Sabrina's house.

Time enough to think of the best possible way to give them the scare of their lives.

I don't want to just jump out at them, Carly Beth thought, playing her fingers over the sharp fangs. *That's too boring.*

I want to do something they'll remember.

Something they'll never forget.

She ran her hands over the mask's pointy ears. Suddenly, she had an idea.

Carly Beth pulled the old broom handle from the closet. She brushed off a thick ball of dust and examined the long wooden pole.

Perfect, she thought.

She checked to make sure her mother was still in the kitchen. She was sure that her mother wouldn't approve of what Carly Beth was about to do. Mrs. Caldwell still thought that Carly Beth was going to wear the duck costume.

Tiptoeing silently into the living room, Carly Beth stepped up to the mantel and pulled down the plaster of Paris head her mother had sculpted.

It really does look just like me, Carly Beth thought, holding the sculpture waist high and studying it carefully. *It's so lifelike. Mom is really talented.*

Carefully, she placed the head on the broomstick. It balanced easily.

She carried it over to the hallway mirror. *It looks like I'm carrying my real head on a stick,*

Carly Beth thought, admiring it. A wide grin broke out across her face. Her eyes sparkled gleefully.

Excellent!

She leaned the head and stick against the wall and pulled on the mask. Once again, the sour aroma rushed into her nostrils. The heat of the mask seemed to wrap around her.

The mask tightened against her skin as she pulled it down.

Raising her eyes to the mirror, she nearly frightened *herself! It's like a real face,* she thought, unable to take her eyes away. *My eyes seem a part of it. It doesn't look as if I'm peering out of eyeholes.*

She moved the gruesome mouth up and down a few times. *It moves like a real mouth,* she realized.

It doesn't look like a mask at all.

It looks like a gross, deformed face.

Working with both hands, she flattened the bulging forehead, smoothing it over her hair.

Excellent! she repeated to herself, feeling her excitement grow. *Excellent!*

The mask is perfect! she decided. She couldn't believe the man in the party store didn't want to sell it to her. It was the scariest, realest, ugliest mask she had ever seen.

I will be the terror of Maple Avenue tonight! Carly Beth decided, admiring herself in the mirror. Kids will be having nightmares about me for weeks!

Especially Chuck and Steve, she told herself.

"Boo!" she muttered to herself, pleased to hear that the gruff voice had returned. "I'm ready."

She picked up the broomstick, carefully balanced her sculpted head on top of it, and started to the door.

Her mother's voice stopped her. "Carly Beth — wait up," Mrs. Caldwell called from the kitchen. "I want to see how you look in that duck costume!"

"Uh-oh," Carly Beth groaned out loud. "Mom isn't going to like this."

Carly Beth froze in the doorway. She could hear her mother's footsteps approaching in the hallway.

"Let me see you, dear," Mrs. Caldwell called. "Did the costume fit?"

Maybe I should've told her about my change of plans, Carly Beth thought guiltily. *I would've said something, but I didn't want to hurt Mom's feelings.*

Now she's in for a shock. And she's going to be really angry when she sees I've borrowed her sculpture.

She's going to make me put it back on the mantel.

She's going to ruin everything.

"I'm kind of in a hurry, Mom," Carly Beth called, her voice deep and raspy inside the mask. "I'll see you later, okay?" She pulled open the front door.

"You can wait one second while I see my costume on you," her mother called. She rounded the corner and came into view.

I'm sunk, Carly Beth thought with a groan. *I'm caught.*

The phone rang. The sound echoed loudly inside Carly Beth's mask.

Her mother stopped and turned back to the kitchen. "Oh, darn. I'd better answer that. It's probably your father calling from Chicago." She disappeared back to the kitchen. "I'll have to see you later, Carly Beth. Be careful, okay?"

Carly Beth breathed a sigh of relief. *Saved by the bell*, she thought.

Balancing the head on the broomstick, she hurried out the door. She closed the door behind her and jogged down the front yard.

It had become a clear, cool night. A pale half-moon rose low over the bare trees. Fat brown leaves swirled around her ankles as she headed to the sidewalk.

The plan was to meet Chuck and Steve in front of Sabrina's house. Carly Beth couldn't wait.

Her head bobbed and bounced on the broom-stick as she ran. The house on the corner had been decorated for Halloween. Orange lights ran along the top of the stoop. Two large smiling pumpkin cutouts stood beside the doorway. A cardboard skeleton had been propped up at the end of the front walk.

I love Halloween! Carly Beth thought happily. She crossed the street onto Sabrina's block.

On other Halloween nights, she had been frightened. Her friends were always playing mean tricks on her. Last year, Steve had slipped a very real-looking rubber rat into her trick-or-treat bag.

When Carly Beth had reached into the bag, she felt something soft and hairy. She pulled out the rat and shrieked at the top of her lungs. She was so scared, she spilled her candy all over the driveway.

Chuck and Steve thought it was a riot. So did Sabrina. They always spoiled Halloween for her. They thought it was so hilarious to scare Carly Beth and make her scream.

Well, this year I won't be the one screaming, she thought. *This year, I'll be the one making everyone else scream.*

Sabrina's house was at the end of the block. As Carly Beth hurried toward it, bare tree limbs shivered above her. The half-moon disappeared behind a heavy cloud, and the ground darkened.

The head on the broom handle bounced and nearly fell off. Carly Beth slowed her pace. She glanced up at the head, shifting her grip on the broomstick.

The eyes on the sculpted head stared straight ahead, as if watching out for trouble. In the darkness, the head looked real. The shadows moving over it as Carly Beth walked under the bare tree limbs made the eyes and mouth appear to move.

Hearing laughter, Carly Beth turned. Across the street, a group of trick-or-treaters was invading a brightly lit front porch. In the yellow porchlight, Carly Beth saw a ghost, a Mutant Ninja Turtle, a Freddy Kreuger, and a princess in a pink ballgown and a tinfoil crown. The kids were little. Two mothers watched them from the foot of the driveway.

Carly Beth watched them get their candy. Then she walked the rest of the way to Sabrina's house. She climbed the front stoop, stepping into a white triangle of light from the porchlight. She could hear voices inside the house, Sabrina shouting something to her mother, a TV on in the living room.

Carly Beth adjusted her mask with her free hand. She straightened the gaping fanged mouth. Then she checked to make sure the head was balanced on the broomstick.

She reached to ring Sabrina's doorbell — then stopped.

Voices behind her.

She turned and squinted into the darkness. Two costumed boys were approaching, shoving each other playfully on the sidewalk.

Chuck and Steve!

I'm just in time, Carly Beth thought happily. She leaped off the stoop and crouched behind a low evergreen shrub.

Okay, guys, she thought eagerly, her heart pounding. *Get ready for a scare.*

Carly Beth peered over the top of the shrub. The two boys were halfway up the driveway.

It was too dark to get a good look at their costumes. One of them wore a long overcoat and a wide-brimmed Indiana Jones fedora. She couldn't really see the other one.

Carly Beth took a deep breath and prepared to leap out at them. She gripped the broomstick tightly.

My whole body is trembling, she realized. The mask suddenly felt hot, as if her excitement had heated it up. Her breath rattled noisily in the flat nose.

Walking slowly, playfully blocking each other with their shoulders like football linemen, the boys made their way up the driveway. One of them said something Carly Beth couldn't hear. The other one laughed loudly, a high-pitched giggle.

Peering into the darkness, Carly Beth watched them until they were nearly right in front of the shrub.

Okay — now! she declared silently.

Raising the broomstick with its staring head on the top, she leaped out.

The boys shrieked, startled.

She could see their dark eyes go wide as they gaped at her mask.

A ferocious roar escaped her throat. A deep, rumbling howl that frightened even her.

At the terrifying sound, both boys cried out again. One of them actually dropped to his knees on the driveway.

They both stared up at the head bobbing on the broomstick. It seemed to glare down at them.

Another howl escaped Carly Beth's throat. It started low, as if coming from far away, and then pierced the air, raspy and deep, like the roar of an angry creature.

"Noooo!" one of the boys cried.

"Who *are* you?" the other cried. "Leave us alone!"

Carly Beth heard rapid footsteps crunching over the dead leaves on the driveway. Looking up, she saw a woman in a bulky down coat running up the driveway.

"Hey — what are you doing?" the woman

demanded, her voice shrill and angry. "Are you scaring my kids?"

"Huh?" Carly Beth swallowed hard. She turned her eyes back to the two frightened boys.

"Wait!" she cried, realizing they weren't Chuck and Steve.

"What are you doing?" the woman repeated breathlessly. She stepped up to the two boys and put a hand on each of their shoulders. "Are you two okay?"

"Yeah. We're okay, Mom," the one in the overcoat and fedora replied.

The other boy wore white makeup and a red clown nose. "She — she jumped out at us," he told his mother, avoiding Carly Beth's stare. "She kind of scared us."

The woman turned angrily to Carly Beth and shook her finger at her accusingly. "Don't you have anything better to do than to scare two young boys? Why don't you pick on someone your own age?"

Normally, Carly Beth would have apologized. She would have explained to the woman that she made a mistake, that she meant to scare two different boys.

But hidden behind the ugly mask, still hearing the strange howl that had burst so unexpectedly from her throat, she didn't feel like apologizing.

She felt . . . anger. And she wasn't sure why.

"Go away!" she rasped, waving the broomstick menacingly. The head — *her* head — stared down at the two startled boys.

"What did you say?" their mother demanded, her voice tight with growing outrage. *"What* did you say?"

"I said *go away!"* Carly Beth snarled in a voice so deep, so terrifying, that it frightened even her.

The woman crossed her arms in front of the heavy down coat. Her eyes narrowed on Carly Beth. "Who are you? What is your name?" she demanded. "Do you live around here?"

"Mom — let's just go," the boy with the clown face urged, tugging at her coat sleeve.

"Yeah. Come on," his brother pleaded.

"Go away. I'm WARNING you!" Carly Beth growled.

The woman stood her ground, her arms tightly crossed, her eyes narrowed at Carly Beth. "Just because it's Halloween doesn't give you the right —"

"Mom, we want to get some candy!" the clown pleaded, tugging his mother's sleeve harder. "Come on!"

"We're wasting the whole night!" his brother complained.

Carly Beth was breathing hard, her breath escaping the mask in low, noisy grunts. *I sound like an animal,* she thought, puzzled. *What is happening to me?*

She could feel her anger growing. Her breathing rattled noisily in the tight mask. Her face felt burning hot.

Her anger raged through her chest. Her entire body was trembling. She felt about to burst.

I'm going to tear this woman apart! Carly Beth decided.

I'll chew her to bits! I'll tear her skin off her bones! Furious thoughts raged through Carly Beth's mind.

She tensed her muscles, crouched low, and prepared to pounce.

But before she could make her move, the two boys pulled their mother away.

"Let's go, Mom."

"Yeah. Let's go. She's *crazy!*"

Yeah. I'm crazy. Crazy, crazy, CRAZY. The word repeated, roaring through Carly Beth's mind. The mask grew hotter, tighter.

The woman gave Carly Beth one last cold stare. Then she turned and led the two boys down the driveway.

Carly Beth stared after them, panting loudly. She had a strong urge to chase after them — to *really* scare them!

But a loud cry made her stop and spin around.

Sabrina stood on the front stoop, leaning on the

storm door, her mouth open in a wide O of surprise. "Who's there?" she cried, squinting into the darkness.

Sabrina was dressed as Cat Woman, with a silver-and-gray catsuit and a silver mask. Her black hair was pulled tightly behind her head. Her dark eyes stared intently at Carly Beth.

"Don't you recognize me?" Carly Beth rasped, stepping closer.

She could see the fright in Sabrina's eyes. Sabrina gripped the door handle tightly, standing half in and half out of her house.

"Don't you recognize me, Sabrina?" She waved the head on the broomstick, as if giving her friend a clue.

Sabrina gasped and raised her hand to her mouth as she noticed the head on the pole. "Carly Beth — is that — is that *you*?" she stammered. Her eyes darted from the mask to the head, then back again.

"Hi, Sabrina," Carly Beth growled. "It's me."

Sabrina continued to study her. "That mask!" she cried finally. "It's *excellent*! Really. Excellent. It's so scary."

"I like your catsuit," Carly Beth told her, stepping closer into the light.

Sabrina's eyes were raised to the top of the broomstick. "That head — it's so real! Where did you get it?"

"It's my *real* head!" Carly Beth joked.

Sabrina continued to stare at it. "Carly Beth, when I first saw it, I —"

"My mom made it," Carly Beth told her. "In her art class."

"I thought it was a real head," Sabrina said. She shivered. "The eyes. The way they stare at you."

Carly Beth shook the broomstick, making the head nod.

Sabrina studied Carly Beth's mask. "Wait till Chuck and Steve see your costume."

I can't wait! Carly Beth thought darkly. "Where are they?" she demanded, glancing back to the street.

"Steve called," Sabrina replied. "He said they'd be late. He has to take his little sister trick-or-treating before he can meet us."

Carly Beth sighed, disappointed.

"We'll start without them," Sabrina suggested. "They can catch up to us later."

"Yeah. Okay," Carly Beth replied.

"I'll get my coat and we can go," Sabrina said. She took one last lingering look at the head on the broomstick, then the storm door slammed shut with a *bang* as she disappeared inside to get her coat.

The wind picked up as the two girls made their way down the block. Dead leaves swirled at their feet. The bare trees bent and shivered.

Above the dark, sloping roofs, the pale half-moon slipped in and out of the clouds.

Sabrina chattered about all the problems she'd had with her costume. The first catsuit she'd bought had a long run in one leg and had to be returned. Then Sabrina couldn't find a cat-eyed mask that looked right.

Carly Beth remained quiet. She couldn't hide her disappointment that Chuck and Steve hadn't met them as planned.

What if they never catch up to us? She wondered. *What if we don't see them at all?*

The whole point of the night, as far as Carly Beth was concerned, was meeting the two boys and scaring the living daylights out of them.

Sabrina had given her a shopping bag to put her candy in. As they walked, Carly Beth gripped the bag in one hand, struggling to keep the head balanced on the pole in her other hand.

"So where did you buy your mask? Your mother didn't *make* it, did she? Did you go to that new party store? Can I touch it?"

Sabrina always talked a lot. But tonight she was going for a world's record of nonstop chatter.

Carly Beth obediently stopped so that her friend could touch the mask. Sabrina pressed her fingers against the cheek, then instantly jerked them back.

"Oh! It feels like skin!"

Carly Beth laughed, a scornful laugh she had never heard before.

"Yuck! What's it made of?" Sabrina demanded.

"It isn't skin — *is* it? It's some kind of rubber, right?"

"I guess," Carly Beth muttered.

"Then how come it's so warm?" Sabrina asked. "Is it uncomfortable to wear? You must be sweating like a pig."

Feeling a surge of rage, Carly Beth dropped the bag and the broomstick.

"Shut up! Shut up! Shut up!" she snarled.

Then with an angry howl, she grabbed Sabrina's throat with both hands and began to choke her.

16

Sabrina uttered a shocked cry and staggered back, pulling herself from Carly Beth's grip. "C-Carly Beth!" she sputtered.

What is happening to me? Carly Beth wondered, gaping in horror at her friend. *Why did I do that?*

"Uh . . . gotcha!" Carly Beth exclaimed. She laughed. "You should have seen the look on your face, Sabrina. Did you think I was really choking you?"

Sabrina rubbed her neck with one silver-gloved hand. She frowned at her friend. "That was a joke? You scared me to death!"

Carly Beth laughed again. "Just keeping in character," she said lightly, pointing to her mask. "You know. Trying to get in the right mood. Ha-ha. I *like* scaring people. You know. Usually I'm the one who's trembling in fright."

She picked up the bag and broomstick, fixing the plaster of Paris head on the top. Then she hurried up the nearest driveway toward a well-lighted house with a HAPPY HALLOWEEN banner in the front window.

Does Sabrina believe it was just a joke? Carly Beth asked herself as she raised her shopping bag and rang the doorbell. *What on earth was I doing? Why did I suddenly get so angry? Why did I attack my best friend like that?*

Sabrina stepped up beside her as the front door was pulled open. Two little blond kids, a boy and a girl, appeared in the doorway. Their mother stepped up behind them.

"Trick or Treat!" Carly Beth and Sabrina called out in unison.

"Ooh, that's a scary mask!" the woman said to her two children, grinning at Carly Beth.

"What are you supposed to be? A cat?" the little boy asked Sabrina.

Sabrina meowed at him. "I'm Cat Woman," she told him.

"I don't like the other one!" the little girl exclaimed to her mother. "It's too scary."

"It's just a funny mask," the mother assured her daughter.

"Too scary. It's *scaring* me!" the little girl insisted.

Carly Beth leaned into the entryway of the house, bringing her grotesque face up close to the little girl. "*I'll eat you up!*" she growled nastily.

67

The little girl screamed and disappeared into the house. Her brother stared wide-eyed at Carly Beth. The mother quickly dropped candy bars into the girls' bags. "You shouldn't have scared her," she said softly. "She has nightmares."

Instead of apologizing, Carly Beth turned to the little boy. *"I'll eat you up, too!"* she snarled.

"Hey — stop!" the woman protested.

Carly Beth laughed a deep-throated laugh, jumped off the porch, and took off across the front lawn.

"Why'd you do that?" Sabrina asked as they made their way across the street. "Why'd you scare those kids like that?"

"The mask made me do it," Carly Beth replied. She meant it as a joke. But the thought troubled her mind.

At the next few houses, Carly Beth hung back and let Sabrina do the talking. At one house, a middle-aged man in a torn blue sweater pretended to be scared of Carly Beth's mask. His wife insisted that the girls come inside so that they could show their elderly mother the great costumes.

Carly Beth groaned loudly but followed Sabrina into the house. The old woman gazed at them blankly from her wheelchair. Carly Beth growled at her, but it didn't appear to make any impression.

On their way out the door, the man in the torn

sweater handed each girl a green apple. Carly Beth waited till they were down on the sidewalk. Then she turned, pulled back her arm, and heaved the apple at the man's house with all her might.

It made a loud *thunk* as it smacked against the shingled front wall near the front door.

"I really *hate* getting apples on Halloween!" Carly Beth declared. "Especially green ones!"

"Carly Beth — I'm worried about you!" Sabrina cried, eyeing her friend with concern. "You're not acting like you at all."

No. I'm not a pitiful, frightened little mouse tonight, Carly Beth thought bitterly.

"Give me that," she ordered Sabrina, and grabbed Sabrina's apple from her bag.

"Hey — stop!" Sabrina protested.

But Carly Beth arched her arm and tossed Sabrina's apple at the house. It clanged noisily as it hit the aluminum gutter.

The man in the torn sweater poked his head out the door. "Hey — what's the big idea?"

"Run!" Carly Beth screamed.

The two girls took off, running at full speed down the block. They didn't stop until the house was out of sight.

Sabrina grabbed Carly Beth's shoulders and held on, struggling to catch her breath. "You're crazy!" she gasped. "You're really crazy!"

"It takes one to know one," Carly Beth said playfully.

They both laughed.

Carly Beth searched the block, looking for Chuck and Steve. She saw a small group of costumed kids huddled together at the corner. But no sign of the two boys.

Smaller houses, jammed closer together, lined the two sides of this block. "Let's split up," Carly Beth suggested, leaning against the broomstick. "We'll get more candy that way."

Sabrina frowned at her friend, eyeing her suspiciously. "Carly Beth, you don't even *like* candy!" she exclaimed.

But Carly Beth was already running up the driveway to the first house, her sculpted head bobbing wildly above her on its broomstick.

This is my night, Carly Beth thought, accepting a candy bar from the smiling woman who answered the door. *My night!*

She felt a tingle of excitement she'd never felt before. And a strange feeling she couldn't describe. A hunger . . .

A few minutes later, her shopping bag starting to feel heavy, she came to the end of the block. She hesitated on the corner, trying to decide whether to do the other side of the street or go on to the next block.

It was very dark there, she realized. The moon had once again disappeared behind dark clouds. The corner streetlight was out, probably burned out.

Across the street, four very young trick-or-treaters were giggling as they approached a house with a jack-o'-lantern on the porch.

Carly Beth sank back into the darkness. She heard voices, boys' voices.

Chuck and Steve?

No. The voices were unfamiliar. They were arguing about where to trick-or-treat next. One of them wanted to go home and call a friend.

How about a little scare for you guys? Carly Beth thought, a smile spreading across her face. *How about something to remember this Halloween night?*

She waited, listening, until they were a few feet away. She could see them now. Two mummies, their faces wrapped in gauze.

Closer, closer. She waited for the perfect moment.

Then she burst from the shadows, uttering an angry animal howl that shattered the air.

The two boys gasped and jumped back.

"Hey!" One of them tried to shout, but his voice caught in his throat.

The other one dropped his bag of candy.

As he started to pick it up, Carly Beth moved quickly. She grabbed the bag from his hand, jerked it away from him, and started to run.

"Come back!"

"That's *mine!*"

"Hey —"

Their voices were high and shrill, filled with fear and surprise. As she ran across the street, Carly Beth glanced back to see if they were following her.

No. They were too frightened. They stood huddled together on the corner, shouting after her.

Holding the stolen candy bag tightly in her free hand, Carly Beth tossed back her head and laughed. A cruel laugh, a triumphant laugh. A laugh she had never heard before.

She emptied the boy's candy into her own bag, then tossed his bag onto the ground.

She felt good, really good. Really strong. And ready for more fun.

Come on, Chuck and Steve, she thought. *It's YOUR turn next!*

17

Carly Beth found Chuck and Steve a few minutes later.

They were across the street from her, standing in the light of someone's driveway, examining the contents of their trick-or-treat bags.

Carly Beth ducked behind the wide trunk of an old tree near the sidewalk. Her heart began to pound as she spied on them.

Neither boy had bothered to put on a real costume. Chuck had a red bandanna tied around his head and a black mask over his eyes. Steve had blackened his cheeks and forehead with big smudges and wore an old tennis hat and a torn raincoat.

Is he supposed to be a bum? Carly Beth wondered.

She watched them sift through their bags. They had been out for quite a while, she saw. Their bags appeared pretty full.

Suddenly, Steve glanced up in her direction.

Carly Beth jerked her head back behind the tree trunk.

Had he seen her?

No.

Don't blow it now, she told herself. *You've waited so long for this moment. You've waited so long to pay them back for all the scares.*

Carly Beth watched the two boys make their way up to the front porch of the next house. Nearly tripping over the broomstick, she darted away from the tree. She ran across the street and ducked low behind a hedge.

When they come back down the driveway, I'll leap out. I'll pounce on them. I'll scare them to death, she thought.

The low hedge smelled piney and sweet. It was still wet from the morning's rain. The wind made the leaves tremble. What was that strange whistling sound?

It took Carly Beth a while to realize it was her own breathing.

She suddenly began to have doubts.

This isn't going to work, she thought, crouching lower behind the trembling hedge.

I am a complete jerk. Chuck and Steve aren't going to be scared by a stupid mask.

I'm going to jump out at them, and they're going to laugh at me. As they always do.

They're going to laugh and say, "Oh, hi, Carly Beth. Looking good!" Or something like that.

74

And then they'll tell everyone in school how I thought I was so scary and how they recognized me immediately and what a total jerk I am. And everyone will have a good laugh at my expense. Why did I ever think this would work? What made me think it was such a hot idea?

Crouched behind the hedge, Carly Beth could feel her anger grow. Anger at herself. Anger at the two boys.

Her face felt burning hot inside the ugly mask. Her heart thudded loudly. Her rapid breaths whistled against the flat nose.

Chuck and Steve were approaching. She could hear their sneakers crunch over the gravel driveway.

Carly Beth tensed her leg muscles and prepared to pounce.

Okay, she thought, taking a deep breath, *here goes!*

It all seemed to happen in slow motion.

The two boys moved slowly past the hedge. They were talking excitedly to each other. But to Carly Beth, their voices seemed low and far away.

She pulled herself up, stepped out from the hedge, and screamed at the top of her lungs.

Even in the dim light, she could see their reactions clearly.

Their eyes went wide. Their mouths dropped open. Their hands shot up above their heads.

Steve cried out. Chuck grabbed the sleeve of Steve's coat.

Carly Beth's scream echoed over the dark front lawn. The sound seemed to hover in the air.

Everything moved so slowly. So slowly, Carly Beth could see Chuck's eyebrows quiver. She could see his chin tremble.

She could see the fear shimmer in Steve's eyes as they moved from her mask up to the head on the broomstick.

She waved the broomstick menacingly.

Steve uttered a frightened whimper.

Chuck gaped at Carly Beth, his frightened eyes locked on hers. "Carly Beth — is that *you?*" he finally managed to choke out.

Carly Beth uttered an animal growl but didn't reply.

"Who *are* you?" Steve demanded, his voice trembling.

"It — it's Carly Beth — I think!" Chuck told him. "Is it you in there, Carly Beth?"

Steve let out a tense laugh. "You — scared us!"

"Carly Beth — is it you?" Chuck demanded again.

Carly Beth waved the broomstick. She pointed up to the head. "That's Carly Beth's head," she told them. Her voice was a deep, throaty rasp.

"Huh?" Both boys gazed up at it uncertainly.

"That's Carly Beth's head," she repeated slowly, waving it toward them. The painted eyes of the sculpted face appeared to glare down at them. "Poor Carly Beth didn't want to give up her head tonight. But I took it anyway."

Both boys stared up at the head.

Chuck continued to grip Steve's coat sleeve.

Steve uttered another tense laugh. He stared at Carly Beth, his expression confused. "You're Carly Beth, right? How are you making that weird voice?"

"That's your friend Carly Beth," she growled,

pointing up to the head on the broomstick. "That's all that's left of her!"

Chuck swallowed hard. His eyes were trained on the bobbing head. Steve stared intently at Carly Beth's mask.

"Hand over your candy," Carly Beth snarled, surprised by the vicious tone in her voice.

"Huh?" Steve cried.

"Hand it over. Now. Or I'll put your heads on the stick."

Both boys laughed, shrill giggles.

"I'm not joking!" Carly Beth roared.

Her angry words cut their laughter short.

"Carly Beth — give us a break," Chuck muttered uncertainly, his eyes still narrowed in fear.

"Yeah. Really," Steve said softly.

"Hand over your bags," Carly Beth insisted coldly. "Or your heads will adorn my stick."

She lowered the broomstick toward them menacingly.

And as she lowered it, all three of them stared up at the dark-eyed face. All three of them studied the frozen face, the face that looked so real, that looked so much like Carly Beth Caldwell.

A sudden breeze swirled around them, making the head bob on the stick.

And then, all three of them saw the eyes blink.

Once. Twice.

The brown eyes blinked.

And the lips on the head parted, making a dry scraping sound.

Frozen in horror, Carly Beth stared up at the face along with the two boys.

And all three of them saw the lips move. And heard the dry, crackling sound.

All three of them saw the dark lips squeeze together, then part.

All three of them saw the bobbing head form the silent words: *"Help me. Help me."*

In her horror, Carly Beth let go of the broomstick. It hit the ground beside Chuck. The head rolled under the hedge.

"It — it *talked!*" Steve cried.

Chuck uttered a low whimper.

Without another word, both boys dropped their candy bags and took off, their sneakers thudding loudly on the sidewalk.

The wind swirled around Carly Beth as if holding her in place.

She felt like tossing her head back and howling.

She felt like tearing off her coat and flying through the night.

She felt like climbing a tree, leaping onto a roof, roaring up at the starless black sky.

She stood frozen for a long moment, letting the wind sweep around her. The boys were gone. They had fled in terror.

Terror!

Carly Beth had succeeded. She had scared them nearly to death.

She knew she'd never forget the horrified looks on their faces, the fear and disbelief that glowed in their dark eyes.

And she would never forget her feeling of triumph. The thrilling sweetness of revenge.

For a brief moment, she realized, she had felt the fear, too.

She had imagined that the head on the stick had come to life, had blinked its eyes, had spoken silently to them.

For a brief moment, she had caught the fear. She had fallen under the spell of her own trickery.

But, of course, the head hadn't come alive, she assured herself now. Of course the lips hadn't moved, hadn't made their silent plea: *"Help me. Help me."*

It had to be shadows, she knew. Shadows cast by the light of the moon, floating out from behind the shifting black clouds.

Where was the head?

Where was the broomstick she had dropped?

It didn't matter now. They were no longer of any use to her.

Carly Beth had won her victory.

And now she was running. Running wildly over the front lawns. Jumping over shrubs and hedges. Flying over the dark, hard ground.

She was running blindly, the houses whirring past on both sides. The blustery wind swirled, and she swirled with it, rising over the sidewalks, rushing through tall weeds, blowing with the wind like a helpless leaf.

Holding her bulging candy bag, she ran past startled trick-or-treaters, past glowing pumpkins, past rattling skeletons.

She ran until her breath gave out.

Then she stopped, panting loudly, and shut her eyes, waiting for her heart to stop pounding, for the blood to stop pulsing at her temples.

And a hand grabbed her shoulder roughly from behind.

Startled, Carly Beth shrieked and spun around. "Sabrina!" she cried breathlessly.

Grinning, Sabrina let go of her shoulder. "I've been looking for you for hours," Sabrina scolded. "Where'd you go?"

"I — I guess I got lost," Carly Beth replied, still struggling to catch her breath.

"One minute you were there. The next minute, you disappeared," Sabrina said, adjusting her mask over her dark hair.

"How'd you do?" Carly Beth asked, trying to speak in her normal voice.

"I ripped my catsuit," Sabrina complained, frowning. She pulled at the Lycra material on one leg to show Carly Beth. "Snagged it on a stupid mailbox."

"Bad news," Carly Beth sympathized.

"Did you scare anyone with that mask?" Sabrina demanded, still fingering the tear in the catsuit leg.

"Yeah. A few kids," Carly Beth replied casually.

"It's really gross," Sabrina said.

"That's why I picked it."

They both laughed.

"Did you get a lot of candy?" Sabrina asked. She picked up Carly Beth's bag and looked inside. "Wow! What a haul!"

"I hit a lot of houses," Carly Beth said.

"Let's go back to my house and check out the loot," Sabrina suggested.

"Yeah. Okay." Carly Beth followed her friend across the street.

"Unless you want to trick-or-treat some more," Sabrina offered, stopping in the middle of the street.

"No. I've done enough," Carly Beth said. She laughed to herself. *I did everything I wanted to do tonight.*

They started walking again. They were walking against the wind, but Carly Beth didn't feel at all chilled.

Two girls in frilly dresses, their faces brightly made up, funny, blond, moplike wigs on their heads, ran by. One of them slowed when she caught sight of Carly Beth's mask. She uttered a soft gasp, then hurried after her friend.

"Did you see Steve and Chuck?" Sabrina asked. "I searched everywhere for them." She groaned. "That's all I did tonight. I spent the whole night looking for everybody. You. Steve and Chuck. How come we never got together?"

Carly Beth shrugged. "I saw them," she told her friend. "A few minutes ago. Back there." She motioned with her head. "They're such scaredy-cats."

"Huh? Steve and Chuck?" Sabrina's expression turned to surprise.

"Yeah. They got one look at my mask and they took off," Carly Beth told her, laughing. "They were screaming like babies."

Sabrina joined in the laughter. "I don't believe it!" she exclaimed. "They always act so tough. And —"

"I called after them, but they just kept running," Carly Beth told her, grinning.

"Weird!" Sabrina declared.

"Yeah. Weird," Carly Beth agreed.

"Did they know it was you?" Sabrina asked.

Carly Beth shrugged. "I don't know. They took one look at me, and they ran like rabbits."

"They told me they planned to scare *you*," Sabrina revealed. "They were going to sneak up behind you and make scary noises or something."

Carly Beth snickered. "It's hard to sneak up behind someone when you're running for your life!"

Sabrina's house came into view. Carly Beth shifted the candy bag to her other hand.

"I got some good stuff," Sabrina said, peering into her bag as she walked. "I had to get a lot. I have to share it with my cousin. She has the flu and couldn't trick-or-treat tonight."

"I'm not sharing any of mine," Carly Beth said. "Noah went out with his pals. He'll probably come home with a year's supply."

"Mrs. Connelly gave cookies and popcorn again this year," Sabrina said, sighing. "I'll just have to throw it all out. Mom won't let me eat anything that isn't wrapped. She's afraid some ghoul will put poison in it. I had to throw out a lot of good stuff last year."

Sabrina knocked on her front door. A few seconds later, her mother opened it and the girls entered. "That's some mask, Carly Beth," she said, studying it. "How'd you girls do?"

"Okay, I think," Sabrina replied.

"Well, just remember —"

"I know. I know, Mom," Sabrina interrupted impatiently. "Throw out everything that isn't wrapped. Even the fruit."

As soon as Mrs. Mason had gone back to the den, the two girls turned over their bags and dumped all the candy onto the living room rug.

"Hey, look — a big Milky Way!" Sabrina declared, pulling it out of the pile. "My favorite!"

"I *hate* these!" Carly Beth said, holding up an enormous blue jawbreaker. "The last time I tried sucking one of these, I cut my tongue to pieces." She tossed it onto Sabrina's pile.

"Thanks a bunch," Sabrina said sarcastically. She tugged off her mask and dropped it onto the carpet. Her face was flushed. She shook out her black hair.

"There. That feels better," Sabrina said. "Wow. That mask was hot." She raised her eyes to Carly Beth. "Don't you want to take off your mask? You must be *boiling* inside it!"

"Yeah. Good idea." Carly Beth had actually forgotten she was wearing a mask.

She reached up with both hands and tugged at the ears. "Ouch!" The mask didn't budge.

She pulled it by the top of the head. Then she tried stretching it out and tugging it from the cheeks.

"Ouch!"

"What's wrong?" Sabrina asked, concentrating on sorting her candy into piles.

Carly Beth didn't reply. She tried prying the mask off at the neck. Then she tugged it up by the ears again.

"Carly Beth — what's wrong?" Sabrina asked, looking up from her candy.

"Help me!" Carly Beth pleaded in a shrill, frightened voice. "Please — help me! The mask — it won't come off!"

21

On her knees on the carpet, Sabrina glanced up from her piles of candy bars. "Carly Beth, stop clowning around."

"I'm not!" Carly Beth insisted, her voice shrill with panic.

"Aren't you tired of scaring people tonight?" Sabrina demanded. She picked up a clear plastic bag of candy corn. "Wonder if Mom will let me keep this. It's wrapped."

"I'm not trying to scare you. I'm serious!" Carly Beth cried. She tugged at the ears of the mask but couldn't get a good grip.

Sabrina tossed down the bag of candy corn and climbed to her feet. "You really can't get the mask off?"

Carly Beth pulled hard on the chin. "Ouch!" She cried out in pain. "It — it's stuck to my skin or something. Help me."

Sabrina laughed. "We're going to look pretty

88

stupid if we have to call the fire department to get you out of your mask!"

Carly Beth didn't find it funny. She gripped the top of the mask with both hands and pulled with all her strength. The mask didn't budge.

Sabrina's grin faded. She stepped over to her friend. "You're not goofing — *are* you. You're really stuck."

Carly Beth nodded. "Well, come on," she urged impatiently. "Help me pull it off."

Sabrina grabbed the mask top. "It's so warm!" she exclaimed. "You must be suffocating in there."

"Just pull!" Carly Beth wailed.

Sabrina pulled

"Ouch! Not so hard!" Carly Beth cried. "It really hurts!"

Sabrina pulled more gently, but the mask didn't budge. She lowered her hands to the cheeks and pulled.

"Ouch!" Carly Beth shrieked. "It's really stuck to my face."

"What's this thing made of?" Sabrina asked, staring intently at the mask. "It doesn't feel like rubber. It feels like skin."

"I don't know what it's made of, and I don't care," Carly Beth grumbled. "I just want it off. Maybe we should cut it off. You know. With scissors."

"And wreck the mask?" Sabrina asked.

"I don't care!" Carly Beth exclaimed, tugging furiously on it. "I really don't! I just want out! If I don't get this thing off me, I'm going to lose it. I'm serious!"

Sabrina put a calming hand on her friend's shoulder. "Okay. Okay. One more try. Then we'll cut it off."

She narrowed her eyes as she examined the mask. "I should be able to reach underneath it and pull it away," she said, thinking out loud. "If I slip my hands up through the neck, I can stretch it out and then push it up."

"Well, go ahead. Just hurry!" Carly Beth pleaded.

But Sabrina didn't move. Her dark eyes grew wide, and her mouth dropped open as she studied the mask. She uttered a soft gasp of surprise.

"Sabrina? What's the matter?" Carly Beth demanded.

Sabrina didn't reply. Instead, she ran her fingers over Carly Beth's throat.

Her astonished expression remained frozen on her face. She moved behind Carly Beth and ran her fingers along the back of Carly Beth's neck.

"What *is* it? What's the matter?" Carly Beth demanded shrilly.

Sabrina ran a hand back through her black hair. Her forehead wrinkled in concentration. "Carly

Beth," she said finally, "there's something very weird going on here."

"What? What are you *talking* about?" Carly Beth demanded.

"There's no bottom to the mask."

"Huh?" Carly Beth's hands shot up to her neck. She felt around frantically. "What do you *mean?*"

"There's no line," Sabrina told her in a trembling voice. "There's no line between the mask and your skin. No place to slip my hand in."

"But that's crazy!" Carly Beth cried. She moved her hands to her throat, pushing up the skin, feeling for the bottom of the mask. "That's crazy! Just crazy!"

Sabrina raised her hands to her face, her features tight with horror.

"That's crazy! Crazy!" Carly Beth repeated in a high-pitched, frightened voice.

But as her trembling fingers desperately explored her neck, Carly Beth realized that her friend was right.

There was no longer a bottom to the mask. No place where the mask ended. No opening between the mask and Carly Beth's skin.

The mask had become her face.

Carly Beth's legs trembled as she made her way to the mirror in the front entryway. Her hands still frantically searched her throat as she stepped up to the large rectangular wall mirror and brought her face close to the glass.

"No line!" she cried. "No mask line!"

Sabrina stood a few feet back, her expression troubled. "I — I don't understand it," she muttered, staring at Carly Beth's reflection.

Carly Beth uttered a sharp gasp. "Those aren't my eyes!" she screamed.

"Huh?" Sabrina stepped up beside her, still staring into the mirror.

"Those aren't my eyes!" Carly Beth wailed. "My eyes don't look like that."

"Try to calm down," Sabrina urged softly. "Your eyes —"

"They're not mine! Not mine!" Carly Beth cried, ignoring her friend's plea for calm. "Where are my eyes? Where am *I*? Where am I, Sabrina? This isn't *me* in here!"

"Carly Beth — please calm down!" Sabrina urged. But her voice came out choked and frightened.

"It isn't me!" Carly Beth declared, gaping in open-mouthed horror at her reflection, her hands pressed tightly against the grotesquely wrinkled cheeks of the mask. "It isn't me!"

Sabrina reached out to her friend. But Carly Beth pulled away. With a high-pitched wail, a cry of horror and despair, she flung herself through the hallway. She pulled open the front door, struggling with the lock, sobbing loudly.

"Carly Beth — stop! Come back!"

Ignoring Sabrina's pleas, Carly Beth plunged back into the darkness. The storm door slammed behind her.

As she began to run, she could hear Sabrina's frantic cries from the doorway: "Carly Beth — your coat! Come back! You forgot your coat!"

Carly Beth's sneakers thudded over the hard ground. She ran into the darkness beneath the trees, as if trying to hide, as if trying to keep her hideous face from view.

She reached the sidewalk, turned right, and kept running.

She had no idea where she was going. She only

knew she had to run away from Sabrina, away from the mirror.

She wanted to run away from *herself*, away from her face, the hideous face that had stared back at her in the mirror with those frightening, unfamiliar eyes.

Someone else's eyes. Someone else's eyes in her head.

Only it was no longer her head. It was an ugly green monster head that had attached itself to hers.

Uttering another cry of panic, Carly Beth crossed the street and kept running. The dark trees, black against the starless night sky, swayed and shivered overhead. Houses whirred past, a blur of orange light from their windows.

Into the darkness she ran, breathing noisily through the ugly flat nose. She lowered her smooth green head against the wind and stared at the ground as she ran.

But no matter where she turned her gaze, she saw the mask. She saw the face staring back at her, the ugly puckered skin, the glowing orange eyes, the rows of jagged animal teeth.

My face . . . my face . . .

High-pitched screams startled her from her thoughts.

Carly Beth glanced up to see that she had run into a group of trick-or-treaters. There were six or seven of them, all turned toward her, screaming and pointing.

She opened her mouth wide, revealing the sharp fangs, and growled at them, a deep animal growl.

The growl made them grow silent. They stared hard at her, trying to decide if she was threatening them or only kidding.

"What are *you* supposed to be?" a girl in a red-and-white-ruffled clown costume called to her.

I'm supposed to be ME, but I'm not! Carly Beth thought bitterly.

She ignored the question. Lowering her head, turning away from them, she started to run again.

She could hear them laughing now. They were laughing in relief, she knew, glad she was leaving them.

With a bitter sob, she turned the corner and kept running.

Where am I going? What am I doing? Am I going to keep running forever?

The questions roared through her mind.

She stopped short when the party store came into view.

Of course, she thought. *The party store.*

The strange man in the cape. He will help me. He will know what to do.

The man in the cape will know how to get this mask off.

Feeling a surge of hope, Carly Beth jogged toward the store.

But as she neared it, her hope dimmed as dark as the store window. Through the glass she could see that all the lights were out. The store was as dark as the night. It was closed.

As she stared into the darkened store, a wave of despair swept over Carly Beth.

Her hands raised against the window, she pressed her head against the glass. It felt cool against her hot forehead. The *mask's* hot forehead.

She closed her eyes.

What do I do now? What am I doing to do?

"It's all a bad dream," she murmured out loud. "A bad dream. I'm going to open my eyes now and wake up."

She opened her eyes. She could see her eyes, her glowing orange eyes, reflected in the dark window glass.

She could see her grotesque face staring darkly back at her.

"Noooo!" With a shudder that shook her entire body, Carly Beth slammed her fists against the window.

Why didn't I wear my mother's duck costume?

she asked herself angrily. *Why was I so determined to be the scariest creature that ever roamed on Halloween? Why was I so determined to terrify Chuck and Steve?*

She swallowed hard. *Now I'm going to scare people for the rest of my life.*

As the bitter thoughts rolled through her mind, Carly Beth suddenly became aware of movement inside the store. She saw a dark shadow roll over the floor. She heard footsteps.

The door rattled, then opened a few inches.

The store owner poked his head out. His eyes narrowed as they studied Carly Beth. "I stayed late," he said quietly. "I expected to see you again."

Carly Beth was startled by his calmness. "I — I can't get it off!" she sputtered. She tugged at the top of her head to demonstrate.

"I know," the man said. His expression didn't change. "Come inside." He pushed the door open the rest of the way, then stepped back.

Carly Beth hesitated, then walked quickly into the dark store. It was very warm inside.

The owner turned on a single light above the front counter. He was no longer wearing the cape, Carly Beth saw. He wore black suit pants and a white dress shirt.

"You *knew* I'd come back?" Carly Beth demanded shrilly. The raspy voice she had acquired inside the mask revealed both anger and confusion. "How did you know?"

"I didn't want to sell it to you," he replied, staring at the mask. He shook his head, frowning. "You remember, don't you? You remember that I didn't want to sell it to you?"

"I remember," Carly Beth replied impatiently. "Just help me take it off. Okay? Help me."

He stared hard at her. He didn't reply.

"Help me take it off," Carly Beth insisted, shouting. "I want you to take it off!"

He sighed. "I can't," he told her sadly. "I can't take it off. I'm really sorry."

"Wh-what do you mean?" Carly Beth stammered.

The store owner didn't reply. He turned toward the back of the store and motioned for her to follow him.

"Answer me!" Carly Beth shrieked. "Don't walk away! Answer me! What do you *mean* the mask can't be taken off?"

She followed him into the back room, her heart pounding. He clicked on the light.

Carly Beth blinked in the sudden brightness. The two long shelves of hideous masks came into focus. She saw a bare spot on the shelf where hers had stood.

The grotesque masks all seemed to stare at her. She forced herself to look away from them. "Take this mask off — now!" she demanded, moving to block the store owner's path.

"I can't remove it," he repeated softly, almost sadly.

"Why not?" Carly Beth demanded.

He lowered his voice. "Because it isn't a mask."

Carly Beth gaped at him. She opened her mouth, but no sound came out.

"It isn't a mask," he told her. "It's a real face."

Carly Beth suddenly felt dizzy. The floor tilted. The rows of ugly faces glared at her. All of the bulging, bloodshot, yellow and green eyes seemed to be trained on her.

She pressed her back against the wall and tried to steady herself.

The store owner walked over to the display shelf and gestured to the ugly staring heads. "The Unloved," he said sadly, his voice lowered to a whisper.

"I — I don't understand," Carly Beth managed to choke out.

"These are not masks. They are faces," he explained. "Real faces. I made them. I created them in my lab — real faces."

"But — but they are so ugly —" Carly Beth started. "Why — ?"

"They weren't ugly in the beginning," he interrupted, his voice bitter, his eyes angry. "They were beautiful. And they were alive. But something went wrong. When they were taken out of the lab, they changed. My experiments — my poor heads — were a failure. But I had to keep them alive. I *had* to."

"I — I don't believe it!" Carly Beth exclaimed breathlessly, raising her hands to the sides of her

101

face, her green distorted face. "I don't believe any of it."

"I am telling the truth," the store owner continued, running a finger over one side of his narrow mustache, his eyes burning into Carly Beth's. "I keep them here. I call them The Unloved because no one will ever want to see them. Occasionally, someone wanders into the back room — you, for example — and one of my faces finds a new home. . . ."

"*Nooooo!*" Carly Beth uttered a cry of protest, more an animal wail than a human cry.

She stared at the gnarled, twisted faces on the shelf. The bulging heads, the open wounds, the animal fangs. Monsters! All monsters!

"Take this off!" she screamed, losing control. "Take this off! Take it off!"

She began tearing frantically at her face, trying to pull it off, trying to rip it off in pieces.

"Take it off! Take it off!"

He raised a hand to quiet her. "I am sorry. The face is your face now," he said without expression.

"No!" Carly Beth shrieked again in her new raspy voice. "Take it off! Take it off — NOW!"

She tore at the face. But even in her anger and panic, she knew her actions were useless.

"The face can be removed," the store owner told her, speaking softly.

"Huh?" Carly Beth lowered her hands. She stared hard at him. "What did you say?"

"I said there is one way the face can be removed."

"Yes?" Carly Beth felt a powerful chill run down her back, a chill of hope. "Yes? How? Tell me!" she pleaded. "Please — tell me!"

"I cannot do it for you," he replied, frowning. "But I can tell you how. However, if it ever again attaches itself to you or to another person, it will be forever."

"How do I get it off? Tell me! *Tell me!*" Carly Beth begged. "How do I get it off?"

The light flickered overhead. The rows of bloated, distorted faces continued to stare at Carly Beth.

Monsters, she thought.

It's a room full of monsters waiting to come alive.

And now I'm one of them.

Now I'm a monster, too.

The floorboards creaked as the store owner moved away from the display shelves and came up close to Carly Beth.

"How do I get this off me?" she pleaded. "Tell me. Show me — now!"

"It can only be removed once," he repeated softly. "And it can only be removed by a symbol of love."

She stared at him, waiting for him to continue.

The silence filled the room. Heavy silence.

"I — I don't understand," Carly Beth stammered finally. "You've *got* to help me. I don't understand you! Tell me something that makes sense! *Help* me!"

"I can say no more," he said, lowering his head, shutting his eyes, and wearily rubbing his eyelids with his fingers.

"But — what do you *mean* by a symbol of love?" Carly Beth demanded. She grabbed the front of his shirt with both hands. "What do you mean? *What do you mean?*"

He made no attempt to remove her hands. "I can say no more," he repeated in a whisper.

"No!" she shouted. "No! You *have* to help me! You *have* to!"

She could feel her rage explode, could feel herself burst out of control — but she couldn't stop herself.

"I want my face back!" she shrieked, pounding on his chest with both fists. "I want my face back! I want *myself* back!"

She was screaming at the top of her lungs now, but she didn't care.

The store owner backed away, motioning with both hands for her to be quiet. Then, suddenly, his eyes opened wide in fear.

Carly Beth followed his gaze to the display shelves.

"Ohh!" She uttered a startled cry of horror as she saw the rows of faces all begin to move.

Bulging eyes blinked. Swollen tongues licked at dry lips. Dark wounds began to pulsate.

The heads were all bobbing, blinking, *breathing.*

"What — what is happening?" Carly Beth cried in a trembling whisper.

"You've awakened them all!" he cried, his expression as frightened as hers.

"But — but —"

"Run!" he screamed, giving her a hard shove toward the doorway. "Run!"

Carly Beth hesitated. She turned back to stare at the heads bobbing on the shelves.

Fat, dark lips began to move, making wet sucking sounds. Crooked fangs clicked up and down. Ugly inhuman noses twitched and gasped air noisily.

The heads, two long rows of them, throbbed to life.

And the eyes — the blood-veined, bulging eyes — the green eyes, the sickly yellow eyes, the bright scarlet eyes, the disgusting eyeballs hanging by threads — *they were all on her*!

"Run! You've awakened them!" the store owner screamed, his voice choked with fear. "Run! Get *away* from here!"

Carly Beth wanted to run. But her legs wouldn't cooperate. Her knees felt wobbly and weak. She suddenly felt as if she weighed a thousand pounds.

"Run! *Run!*" The store owner repeated his frantic cry.

But she couldn't take her eyes off the throbbing, twitching heads.

Carly Beth gaped at the hideous scene, frozen in terror, feeling her legs turn to Jell-O, feeling her breath catch in her throat. And as she watched, the heads rose up and floated into the air.

"Run! Hurry! Run!"

The store owner's voice seemed far away now.

The heads began to jabber in rumbling, deep voices, drowning out his frantic cries. They murmured excitedly, making only sounds, no words, like a chorus of frogs.

Up, up, they floated, as Carly Beth stared in silent horror.

"Run! Run!"

Yes.

She turned. She forced her legs to move.

And with a burst of energy, she began to run.

She ran through the dimly lit front room of the store. Her hands grabbed for the doorknob, and she pulled open the door.

A second later, she was out on the sidewalk, running through the darkness. Her sneakers thudded loudly on the pavement. She felt a shock of cold air against her hot face.

Her hot green face.

Her monster face.

The monster face she could not remove.

She crossed the street and kept running.

What was that sound? That deep, gurgling sound? That low murmur that seemed to be following her?

Following her?

"Oh, no!" Carly Beth cried out as she glanced back — and saw the gruesome heads flying after her.

A ghoulish parade.

They flew in single file, one long chain of throbbing, jabbering heads. Their eyes glowed brightly, as bright as car headlights, and they were all trained on Carly Beth.

Choked with fear, Carly Beth stumbled over the curb.

Her arms shot forward as she struggled to regain her balance. Her legs wanted to collapse, but she forced them to move again.

Bent into the wind, she ran past dark houses and empty lots.

It must be late, she realized. *It must be very late.*

Too late.

The words flashed into her mind.

Too late for me.

The hideous glowing heads flew after her. Getting closer. Closer. The rumbling of their animal murmurs grew louder in her ears until the frightening sound seemed to surround her.

The wind roared, gusting hard, as if deliberately pushing her back.

The murmuring heads floated closer.

I'm running through a dark nightmare, she thought.

I may run forever.

Too late. Too late for me.

Or *was* it?

An idea formed its way through her nightmarish panic. As she ran, her arms thrashing the air in front of her as if reaching for safety, her mind struggled for a solution, an escape.

A symbol of love.

She heard the store owner's words over the rumble of ugly voices behind her.

A symbol of love.

That's what it would take to rid her of the monster head that had become her own.

Would it also stop the throbbing, glowing heads that pursued her? Would it send the faces of The Unloved back to where they came from?

Gasping loudly for breath, Carly Beth turned the corner and kept running. Glancing back, she could see her chattering pursuers turn, too.

Where am *I*? she wondered, turning her eyes to the houses she was passing.

She had been too frightened to care where she ran.

But now, Carly Beth had an idea. A desperate idea.

And she had to get there before the gruesome parade of heads caught up with her.

She *had* a symbol of love.

It was her head. The plaster of Paris head her mother had sculpted of her.

Carly Beth remembered asking her mother why she had sculpted it. And her mother had replied, "Because I love you." Maybe it could save her. Maybe it could help her out of this nightmare.

But where was it?

She had tossed it aside. She had let it fall behind a hedge. She had left it in someone's yard, and —

And now she was back on the block.

She recognized the street. She recognized the houses.

This was where she had met up with Chuck and Steve. This is where she had sent them running off in terror.

But where was the house? Where was the hedge?

Her eyes darted frantically from yard to yard.

Behind her, she saw, the heads had swarmed together. Like buzzing bees, they had bunched together, grinning now, grinning hideous, wet grins as they prepared to close in on her.

I've got to find the head! Carly Beth told herself, struggling to breathe, struggling to keep her aching legs moving.

I've got to find my head.

The rumbling, jabbering voices grew louder. The heads swarmed closer.

"Where? Where?" she screamed aloud.

And then she saw the tall hedge. Across the street.

The yard across the street.

The head, the beautiful head — she had let it fall behind that hedge.

Could she get to it before the ugly heads swarmed over her?

Yes!

Sucking in a deep breath of air, her arms reaching out desperately in front of her, she turned and ran across the street.

And dove behind the hedge. Onto her hands and knees. Her chest heaving. Her breath rasping. Her head pounding.

She reached for the head.

It was gone.

Gone.

The head was gone.

My last chance, Carly Beth thought, searching blindly, her hand thrashing frantically through the bottom of the hedge.

Gone.

Too late for me.

Still on her knees, she turned to face her ghoulish pursuers. The heads, jabbering their mindless sounds, rose up in front of her, forming a wall.

Carly Beth started to her feet.

The throbbing wall of monster heads inched closer.

She turned, searching for an escape route.

And saw it.

Saw her head.

Saw the plaster of Paris head staring up at her from between two upraised roots on the big tree near the driveway.

The wind must have blown it over there, she realized.

And as the ugly heads bobbed closer, she dove for the tree. And grabbed the head with both hands.

With a cry of triumph, she turned the sculpted face toward the jabbering heads and raised it high.

"Go away! Go away!" Carly Beth screamed, holding the head up so they could all see it. "This is a symbol of love! This is a symbol of love! Go away!"

The heads bobbed together. The glowing eyes stared at the sculpted head.

They murmured excitedly. Wet smiles formed on their distorted lips.

"Go away! Go away!"

Carly Beth heard them laugh. Low, scornful laughter.

Then they moved quickly, surrounding her, eager to swallow her up.

Too late for me.

The words repeated in Carly Beth's mind.

Her idea had failed.

The heads swarmed around her, drooled over her, eyes bulging gleefully in triumph.

Their rumbling murmurs became a roar. She felt herself being swallowed up in their foul-smelling heat.

Without thinking, she lowered the sculpted head. And pulled it down hard over her hideous monster head.

To her surprise, it slid over her like a mask.

I'm wearing my own face like a mask, she thought bitterly.

As she pulled it over her, darkness descended.

There were no eyeholes. She couldn't see out.

She couldn't hear.

What will the gruesome heads do to me? she wondered, alone with her fear.

Will I become one of The Unloved now?

Will I end up on display on a shelf along with them?

Surrounded by the tight, silent darkness, Carly Beth waited.

And waited.

She could feel the blood pulsing at her temples. She could feel the throb of fear in her chest, the ache of her dry throat.

What are they going to do?

What are they doing?

She couldn't bear being alone, shut in with her fear, surrounded by silence and the dark.

With a hard tug, she pulled off the sculpted head.

The gruesome heads were gone.

Vanished.

Carly Beth stared straight ahead in disbelief. Then her eyes darted around the shadowy lawn. She searched the trees and shrubs. She squinted into the dark spaces between the houses.

Gone.

They were gone.

For a long moment, Carly Beth sat in the cold, wet grass, the sculpted head in her lap, breathing hard, staring across the silent, empty front yards.

Soon her breathing returned to normal. She climbed to her feet.

The wind had gentled. The pale half-moon slipped out from behind the dark clouds that had covered it.

Carly Beth felt something flap against her throat.

Startled, she reached up and felt the bottom of the mask.

The bottom of the mask?

Yes!

There was a gap between the mask and her neck.

"Hey!" she cried aloud. Setting the sculpted head down gently at her feet, she raised both hands to the bottom of the mask and pulled up.

The mask came off easily.

Stunned, she lowered it and held it in front of her. She folded it up, then unfolded it.

The orange eyes that had glowed like fire had faded. The pointed animal fangs had become rubbery and limp.

"You're just a mask!" she cried aloud. "Just a mask again!"

Laughing gleefully, she tossed it up in the air and caught it.

It can be removed only once, the store owner had told her.

Only once by a symbol of love.

Well, I've done it! Carly Beth told herself happily. *I've removed it. And don't worry — I'll never put it on again!*

Never!

She suddenly felt exhausted.

I've got to get home, she told herself. *It's probably close to midnight.*

Most of the houses were dark. There were no cars moving on the streets. The trick-or-treaters had all gone home.

Carly Beth bent to pick up the sculpted head. Then, carrying the mask and the plaster head, she began walking quickly toward her house.

Halfway up the driveway, she stopped.

She reached up and examined her face with one hand.

Do I have my old face back? she wondered.

She rubbed her cheeks, then ran her fingers over her nose.

Is it my old face? Do I look like me?

She couldn't tell just by touching.

"I've got to get to a mirror!" she exclaimed out loud.

Desperate to see if her face had returned to normal, she ran up to her front door and rang the bell.

After a few seconds, the door swung open and Noah appeared. He pushed open the storm door.

Then he raised his eyes to her face — and started to scream.

"Take off that mask! Take it off! You're so ugly!!"

"No!" Carly Beth cried in horror.

The mask must have changed her face, she realized.

"No! Oh, no!"

She pushed past her brother, tossed down the head and the mask, and ran to the hallway mirror.

Her face stared back at her.

Perfectly normal. Her old face. Her good old face.

Her dark brown eyes. Her broad forehead. Her snip of a nose, which she had always wished was longer.

I'll never complain about my nose again, she thought happily.

Her face was normal again. All normal.

As she stared at herself, she could hear Noah laughing at the doorway.

She spun around angrily. "Noah — how *could* you?"

He laughed harder. "It was just a joke. I can't believe you fell for it."

"It was no joke to me!" Carly Beth exclaimed angrily.

Her mother appeared at the end of the hall. "Carly Beth, where have you been? I expected you back an hour ago."

"Sorry, Mom," Carly Beth replied, grinning. *I'm so happy, I may never stop grinning!* she thought.

"It's sort of a long story," she told her mother. "Sort of a long, weird story."

"But you're okay?" Mrs. Caldwell's eyes narrowed as she studied her daughter.

"Yeah. I'm okay," Carly Beth said.

"Come into the kitchen," Mrs. Caldwell instructed her. "I have some nice hot cider for you."

Carly Beth obediently followed her mother to the kitchen. The kitchen was warm and bright. The sweet cider aroma filled the room.

Carly Beth had never been so glad to be home in all her life. She hugged her mother, then took a seat at the counter.

"Why didn't you wear your duck costume?" Mrs. Caldwell asked, pouring out a cup of steaming cider. "Where have you been? Why weren't you with Sabrina? Sabrina has called twice already, wondering what happened to you."

"Well . . ." Carly Beth began. "It's sort of a long story, Mom."

"I'm not going anywhere," her mother said, setting the cup of cider down in front of Carly Beth. She leaned against the counter, resting her chin in one hand. "Go ahead. Talk."

"Well . . ." Carly Beth hesitated. "Everything is fine now, Mom. Perfectly fine. But —"

Before she could say another word, Noah burst into the room.

"Hey, Carly Beth —" he called in a deep, raspy voice. "Look at me! How do I look in your mask?"

Read the biography of the man behind the scares, R.L. Stine!

HERE'S A SNEAK PEEK!

ONE

"I MADE MY MOST IMPORTANT DISCOVERY

WHEN I WAS SEVEN . . . "

I was born October 8, 1943, in Columbus, Ohio. My parents called me Robert Lawrence Stine (now you know what the R.L. stands for). One of my earliest memories is a scary one. It's about Whitey.

Whitey was our dog. In pictures, Whitey looks like he was half husky, half collie, and half elephant. He was so big that when we allowed him in the house, he knocked over vases—and the tables they were on! That's why we kept him in the garage.

When I was four, it was my job to let Whitey out of the garage every morning. As soon as I stepped outside, I could hear him scratching at the inside of the garage door.

Slowly, I'd push up the heavy door. And Whitey would come charging out at me. His tail would wag furiously and he would bark like crazy. He was so glad to see me!

Barking and crying, he would leap on me—and knock me to the driveway. Every morning!

"Down, Whitey! Down!" I begged.

THUD! I was down on the driveway.

THUD! Every morning.

Whitey was a good dog. But I think he helped give me my scary view of life. I wonder if I would have become a horror writer if I didn't start every morning when I was four flat on my back on the driveway!

I grew up in the town of Bexley. Bexley is a suburb of Columbus, and Columbus is right in the middle of Ohio.

When I was little, we lived in a three-story house. We had a big yard with a lot of shade trees.

My brother, Bill, is three years younger than me. He and I shared a bedroom on the second floor. The third floor was an attic. It was strictly forbidden. Mom told us never to go up there.

I asked her why. She only shook her head and said, "Don't ask."

That attic from my childhood is also one of the reasons why I write Goosebumps and Fear Street today.

I used to lie in my bed at night and stare at the ceiling. *What terrible thing is up there in the attic?* I wondered. I pretended I could see through the plaster. Of course I couldn't see anything. Except plaster. But my imagination sure could.

In my imagination, a coatrack stood at the top of the attic stairs. Next to it, a three-legged table, several cardboard cartons, and an old windup

"TWO WEEKS OLD, WITH MY MOM.
I'M THE ONE WEARING THE DRESS."

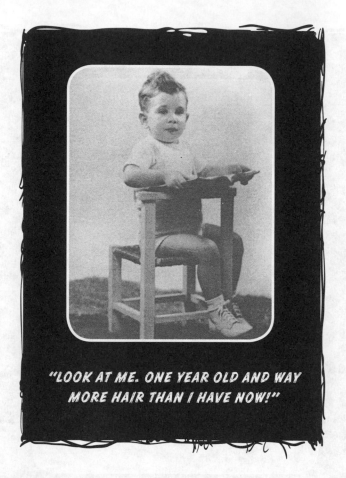

"LOOK AT ME. ONE YEAR OLD AND WAY MORE HAIR THAN I HAVE NOW!"

record player. That dark shape back in the corner was a mysterious old trunk. Oh, and there was a dusty moose head. I could see this stuff as clear as day. But it was only furniture. It wasn't scary.

The scary part was the monster in the attic. I made it up. And I made up stories about the monster with trunks and moose heads. These stories seem silly to me now, but at the time they were the best answer I could come up with to the question, *What's in the attic?*

I knew it had to be something truly awful. Otherwise my mom wouldn't make such a big deal about it.

So I didn't go up to the attic. Not right away. This doesn't mean I had a weird, haunted childhood. I didn't.

My family was a typical family. Dad worked for a restaurant supply company, and Mom was a housewife. We didn't have much money. But my parents worked hard to make sure we never felt poor. There were three of us kids—me, Bill, and my sister, Pam, who came along when I was seven.

My favorite activity as a kid?

Listening to the radio. Believe it or not, we didn't get a TV until I was nine. So I spent hours and hours listening to the radio.

When I was a kid, radio wasn't just music and talk shows. There were wonderful stories, mysteries, comedies, and westerns on the radio every night. I would listen to such exciting shows as *The Lone Ranger*, *The Shadow*, *The Whistler*, and *Gang Busters*.

There was one show that *terrified* me. It was called *Suspense*. I still remember how scary it was.

About the Author

R.L. Stine's books are read all over the world. So far, his books have sold more than 300 million copies, making him one of the most popular children's authors in history. Besides Goosebumps, R.L. Stine has written the teen series Fear Street, the funny series Rotten School, as well as the Mostly Ghostly series, The Nightmare Room series, and the two-book thriller *Dangerous Girls*. R.L. Stine lives in New York with his wife, Jane, and Minnie, his King Charles spaniel. You can learn more about him at www.RLStine.com.

THE ORIGINAL Goosebumps BOOKS
WITH AN ALL-NEW LOOK!

NOW A MAJOR MOTION PICTURE

Goosebumps

A SHOCKER ON SHOCK STREET

R.L. STINE

SCHOLASTIC

NOW A MAJOR MOTION PICTURE

Goosebumps

LET'S GET INVISIBLE!

R.L. STINE

SCHOLASTIC

NOW A MAJOR MOTION PICTURE

Goosebumps

NIGHT OF THE LIVING DUMMY 2

R.L. STINE

SCHOLASTIC

NOW A MAJOR MOTION PICTURE

Goosebumps

NIGHT OF THE LIVING DUMMY 3

R.L. STINE

SCHOLASTIC

NOW A MAJOR MOTION PICTURE

Goosebumps

THE ABOMINABLE SNOWMAN OF PASADENA

R.L. STINE

SCHOLASTIC

NOW A MAJOR MOTION PICTURE

Goosebumps

THE BLOB THAT ATE EVERYONE

R.L. STINE

SCHOLASTIC

NOW A MAJOR MOTION PICTURE

Goosebumps

THE GHOST NEXT DOOR

R.L. STINE

SCHOLASTIC

NOW A MAJOR MOTION PICTURE

Goosebumps

THE HAUNTED CAR

R.L. STINE

SCHOLASTIC

NOW A MAJOR MOTION PICTURE

Goosebumps

ATTACK OF the GRAVEYARD GHOULS

R.L. STINE

SCHOLASTIC

NOW A MAJOR MOTION PICTURE

Goosebumps

A GIVE YOURSELF GOOSEBUMPS BOOK

PLEASE DON'T FEED the VAMPIRE!

R.L. STINE

SCHOLASTIC

IT CAME FROM OHIO!
MY LIFE AS A WRITER

R.L. STINE

A biography of the author of Goosebumps

SCHOLASTIC

R.L. Stine's Biography

SCHOLASTIC

scholastic.com/goosebumps

GBCLRP1

The Original Bone-Chilling Series

—with Exclusive Author Interviews!

NIGHT of the LIVING DUMMY

R.L. STINE

DEEP TROUBLE

R.L. STINE

MONSTER BLOOD

R.L. STINE

the HAUNTED MASK

R.L. STINE

ONE DAY at HORRORLAND

R.L. STINE

the CURSE of the MUMMY'S TOMB

R.L. STINE

BE CAREFUL WHAT YOU WISH FOR

R.L. STINE

SAY CHEESE and DIE!

R.L. STINE

the HORROR at CAMP JELLYJAM

R.L. STINE

HOW I GOT MY SHRUNKEN HEAD

R.L. STINE

SCHOLASTIC

www.scholastic.com/goosebumps

GBCL22

R. L. Stine's Fright Fest!
Now with Splat Stats and More!

Goosebumps
The WEREWOLF of FEVER SWAMP
R.L. STINE
SCHOLASTIC

Goosebumps
A NIGHT in TERROR TOWER
R.L. STINE
SCHOLASTIC

Goosebumps
WELCOME to DEAD HOUSE
R.L. STINE
SCHOLASTIC

Goosebumps
WELCOME to CAMP NIGHTMARE
R.L. STINE
SCHOLASTIC

Goosebumps
GHOST BEACH
R.L. STINE
SCHOLASTIC

Goosebumps
the SCARECROW WALKS at MIDNIGHT
R.L. STINE
SCHOLASTIC

Goosebumps
YOU CAN'T SCARE ME!
R.L. STINE
SCHOLASTIC

Goosebumps
RETURN OF THE MUMMY
R.L. STINE
SCHOLASTIC

Goosebumps
REVENGE of the LAWN GNOMES
R.L. STINE
SCHOLASTIC

Goosebumps
PHANTOM OF THE AUDITORIUM
R.L. STINE
SCHOLASTIC

Goosebumps
VAMPIRE BREATH
R.L. STINE
SCHOLASTIC

Goosebumps
STAY OUT of the BASEMENT
R.L. STINE
SCHOLASTIC

SCHOLASTIC Read them all!

www.scholastic.com/goosebumps

GBCL22

REVENGE OF THE LIVING DUMMY
R.L. STINE
SCHOLASTIC

CREEP FROM THE DEEP
R.L. STINE
SCHOLASTIC

MONSTER BLOOD FOR BREAKFAST!
R.L. STINE
SCHOLASTIC

THE SCREAM OF THE HAUNTED MASK
R.L. STINE
SCHOLASTIC

DR. MANIAC VS. ROBBY SCHWARTZ
R.L. STINE
SCHOLASTIC

WHO'S YOUR MUMMY?
R.L. STINE
SCHOLASTIC

MY FRIENDS CALL ME MONSTER
R.L. STINE
SCHOLASTIC

SAY CHEESE - AND DIE SCREAMING!
R.L. STINE
SCHOLASTIC

WELCOME TO CAMP SLITHER
R.L. STINE
SCHOLASTIC

THE SCARIEST PLACE ON EARTH!

Catch the MOST WANTED Goosebumps® villains UNDEAD OR ALIVE!

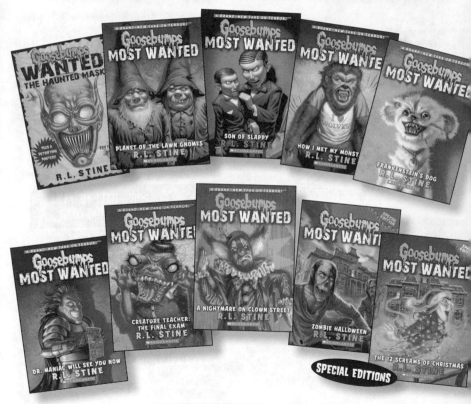